M000159165

TRIAL BY JURY

A RAIN CITY LEGAL THRILLER

STEPHEN PENNER

INKUBATOR
BOOKS

Published by Inkubator Books
www.inkubatorbooks.com

ISBN (eBook): 978-1-83756-232-9
ISBN (Paperback): 978-1-83756-233-6
ISBN (Hardback): 978-1-83756-234-3

1

The judge frowned down from atop the bench. "Any further argument, Mr. Raine?"

Daniel Raine was an attorney; he was always prepared for further argument. But he wasn't paid just to argue. He was paid to win. A glance at the clock confirmed the day was almost over. Judge Kendall, one of the longest serving judges on the King County bench, had already heard everything he needed to make his ruling, and famously harbored little patience for lawyers who spoke just to hear their own voices, a common condition among members of the Bar. Raine knew when to shut up. Also, he had plans for after work.

"No further argument, Your Honor," Raine confirmed. "My client and I await the Court's ruling."

The client was a young woman named Avery Jefferson. She was suing to get sole custody of her children from her abusive, drug-addicted ex-husband. Her ex-husband claimed he didn't have enough money to pay child support but managed to retain one of the top divorce firms in Seattle to try to fool the judge into thinking he had changed his ways. Judge Kendall was about to decide nothing less than whether Avery Jefferson's children would be safe.

"I have listened to your arguments," the judge began, "and I have read your briefs, and all of the cases cited in those briefs. This is an important case with serious allegations and a difficult decision for me to render. The mother asks me to all but terminate the parental rights of the father based on allegations of misconduct which, if true, would certainly support such an extreme decision. The father both denies the allegations but also promises to take steps to address the underlying substance abuse and interpersonal disorders which have led to the behaviors complained of. The easy thing to do would be to split the baby and limit, but not terminate, the residential time of the father. But it's not my job to do the easy thing. My job is to do the right thing."

Raine liked the sound of that.

"Ultimately, I am persuaded by Mr. Raine's advocacy," the judge continued.

Raine really liked the sound of that.

"Mr. Raine pointed out that the father has failed, even in this very hearing, to acknowledge his misdeeds," the judge continued, "but at the same time has promised to take a series of classes designed to address the issues which gave rise to the allegations against him. Still, as Mr. Raine pointed out, a promise is not the same as action. The father has not taken any such courses. Rather he offers to do so if, but only if, the Court finds the allegations of the mother to be true. That is not taking responsibility. That is, as Mr. Raine argued, the exact opposite of taking responsibility."

Raine gave his client a hopeful nod.

She returned it and grabbed onto his hand like a vise.

"Children are a blessing," Judge Kendall concluded, "but they are also a charge. A charge to their parents, of course, but also to this Court, when cases such as this reach my courtroom. The mother's motion for sole custody is granted."

"Yes!" Raine hissed under his breath, pumping a fist out of sight under the table. His joy at winning was increased by the sound of the father ripping into his attorney for having lost the motion.

"We won?" Jefferson asked, eyes wide. "Did we really just win?"

Raine nodded. "We won."

Jefferson wrapped her arms around Raine and squeezed. Raine didn't particularly enjoy receiving hugs from clients, but he enjoyed doing well enough to earn them. "Thank you! Thank you so much."

Raine was reminded to be grateful that he was sharing custody of his own kids with his ex-wife. They had managed to work things out more or less amicably. Then again, the divorce was still fresh. He knew from his job that there was plenty of time for things to turn sour.

Jefferson pulled away and looked up at her lawyer. "Now what? Can we talk about what happens next?"

"Absolutely," Raine glanced at the clock again, "but not right now. Your kids were already with you this week, so they're safe. And I have plans tonight. Call the office and Laura will schedule a meeting as soon as I have some availability."

"What kind of plans could you have on a Tuesday night?" Jefferson questioned.

"Not very good ones," Raine admitted. "But now they're celebration plans. And I'd rather not be late."

'NOT VERY GOOD' was in the eye of the beholder. When Raine arrived, his own trepidation at the evening ahead did not appear to be shared by any of the other guests. In fact, there was an air of excitement and even giddiness floating throughout the space.

The space was The Finch Art Gallery in Seattle's Belltown neighborhood, just north of downtown. The other guests were a collection of artists, art students, art collectors, art dealers, and art lovers. Rebecca Sommers fell into that last category. In addition to being an art lover, she was also a highly successful real estate agent, and, for reasons Raine was still having trouble believing, his private investigator. At least on cases she found interesting. She had eclectic tastes, it seemed. She also had two tickets to a showing at an art gallery owned by one of her many well-to-do friends in Rain City.

The gallery was a delightful space. An installation piece of amber glass of varying sizes and shapes hung from the ceiling, lending a sense of intimacy to contrast with the sharp edges of the bright white angular walls that jutted in and out, providing the space for the dozens, perhaps even hundreds, of works of art on display that evening. Raine had never seen so much art in one place. Then again, he didn't go to art galleries very often. Or ever.

"Dan!" Sommers called out. "Come over here. I want to introduce you to some dear friends of mine."

And that was why Raine had agreed to come to a Tuesday night art show at a gallery far enough away from the courthouse that he needed to drive, even though there was never any parking in Belltown. Sommers had connections, and if Raine was going to grow his law practice after his partner had left to become a judge, he was going to need clients. Rich clients. Sommers's clients. He pasted on a smile and marched dutifully to his partner.

Sommers was dressed in a simple black dress, with leather heels and a brilliant diamond bracelet on each wrist. Her long platinum hair fell loosely over her shoulders and her makeup was perfect. She looked dressed for an evening out. Raine knew she was dressed for work.

He was as well, although his ensemble was hardly as glamorous as hers. He'd come straight from the courthouse, so he was wearing a suit, but it was a workaday suit, with shoes that needed a shine. His tie was new though. Bright red and silk. He felt good about that until he scanned the room and realized that he was the only one there wearing a tie. Seattle was not a formal town.

"Everyone, this is Daniel Raine. He's an attorney, but try not to hold that against him," Sommers began the introductions. She gestured to the woman to her immediate left, an older woman in an expensive-looking ensemble and absolutely laden with diamond jewelry. "Dan, this is Elizabeth Arlington. She's a strong supporter of Seattle's art community."

She's rich. Raine knew what Sommers was really saying.

"Nice to meet you." Raine offered a nod in Arlington's direction.

Arlington returned a reserved smile, but nothing more.

"And this is Caleb Marquardt," Sommers continued around the circle. "Caleb is an art collector."

"Art investor," Marquardt corrected with a toothy grin. He was a very tall man, thin, with curly red hair. "A speculator in the field of creativity, one might say."

One might. Raine probably wouldn't. But he wasn't going to judge the man either. Marquardt made his living off other people's creativity. Raine made his off other people's misery. "Nice to meet you, Caleb."

"And this," Sommers waved her hand dramatically at the last person in their little circle, "is Duncan Finch, the owner and operator of this delightful establishment."

Finch was tall and thin, almost spindly. He had dark blonde hair, grown long in the front and shaved on the sides, with a pair of white-rimmed glasses that mostly obscured the wrinkles starting to form at the corners of his blue eyes.

"Right, The Finch Gallery," Raine noted. He looked around at the vibrant crowd milling about the place. "Congratulations on a successful evening."

But Finch frowned. "Don't be hasty, Daniel. May I call you Daniel?"

Raine doubted he could talk Finch out of it. It had taken far too long to convince Sommers to just call him 'Dan' instead of 'Daniel.' But he didn't get the chance anyway.

"Don't be hasty, Daniel," Finch repeated. "My gallery may be full, but I fear this may turn out to be largely an act of charity. Do you see the crowd here? Do you notice how half of them are too young to drink any of the far-too-expensive champagne being carried around by the caterers I hired? They're art students. All of the art on display this evening is their work. Half-baked works by half-educated art students. I need the other half of the guests to drink enough of that champagne by the end of the evening that they'll open their wallets for paintings no one would ever buy otherwise."

"What happens at the end of the evening?" Raine asked.

"The auction," Sommers explained. "The rich people

spend the evening surveying the paintings, then at the end of the evening, they're auctioned off. A third to the gallery, a third to the school, and a third to starving students who might never get their work in a gallery again, let alone purchased at champagne-fueled prices."

Raine thought that was a nice thing to do for the students. He said as much.

"Duncan is a very generous man." Sommers gave Finch's arm a little squeeze.

"Duncan is a very weak man," Finch responded. "Far too easily talked into doing nice things for other people that may end up costing him money. The caterers I hired weren't cheap."

Raine looked to Sommers. "So, was this your idea?" He'd found Sommers to be the type of person who could talk others into things they might not otherwise want to do.

Sommers laughed lightly. "Oh, no, Dan. I'm here because I'm a friend of Duncan's. And you're here because you're a friend of mine. But we're all here because of that woman right over there."

Sommers pointed into the crowd, toward the far side of the room. Raine hardly expected to be able to discern one person from all the rest, but when he saw her, he knew exactly who Sommers was pointing at. The woman was facing away at first, but turned toward them as Raine watched her. She was tall, with strong shoulders and long auburn-red hair that ended in a torrent of loose curls down her back. She held herself with obvious confidence and was smiling at everyone around her. It was a fantastic smile, white teeth framed by burgundy lips.

"Who is that?" Raine tried not to gasp.

Sommers's chuckle let him know he'd failed. "Selina Thorne."

"She's the director of the Cascadia Art School," Marquardt expounded.

"She's the one who talked me into this financial disaster," Finch concluded.

"Would you like me to introduce you?" Sommers asked.

They both already knew Raine's answer.

Sommers bid the others a temporary farewell, then took Raine by the arm and traversed the crowd until they reached Selina Thorne. Raine found her even more striking up close.

"Selina!" Sommers greeted Thorne as they stepped up. "I'd like to introduce you to my friend and colleague, Daniel Raine. He's a local attorney here in town. Dan, this is Selina Thorne."

Thorne flashed that smile again, but this time directly at Raine. He liked how that made him feel. "Nice to meet you, Mr. Raine. Thank you for coming and supporting my students tonight."

"Call me Daniel," Raine replied, to a raised eyebrow from Sommers. "I'm thrilled to be here. I didn't realize we had so many promising young artists in our community."

"Oh, we have many more than this, Daniel," Thorne told him with a wave at the art-adorned walls surrounding them. "We couldn't even include everyone at Cascadia, let alone all of the other artists in and around Seattle. This isn't even a tip to the enormous iceberg of the creative talent we have hidden all around us."

Raine nodded toward the nearest of those art-adorned walls. "Would you be willing to show me some of the pieces here tonight, Selina? I'm not very artistic myself, but I'm always impressed by the talents of others. And I love to learn new things."

"I would be absolutely delighted to, Daniel," Thorne answered. "Would you care to join us, Rebecca?"

But Sommers grinned at Raine. She could obviously see where the evening was headed. Raine hoped she was right. "No, I think I'll get back to Duncan," Sommers answered. "I'm sure he's wound himself up around some small detail no one else will even notice."

"It was wonderful of him to allow us to do this showing here tonight," Thorne said. "If I'm honest, most of my students may never see their art in an actual gallery. His generosity means more than he knows."

Raine seemed to think Finch was acutely aware of how generous he was being, but he knew better than to say so.

"Please thank Duncan for me," Thorne continued. "I'll catch up with him later to give him my thanks in person as well."

Sommers agreed and left Raine and Thorne to explore the exhibition, alone but together.

"Have you been to many art exhibitions, Daniel?" Thorne asked as she started the tour.

Raine's initial impulse was to lie, which both surprised and bothered him. Lawyers knew a lot about lying. Professional jokes aside, lawyers were used to being lied to by pretty much everyone they encountered, from clients to cops. Raine knew the number one reason people lied was to avoid punishment. The number two reason, he suspected, was men trying to impress women. But Thorne already knew the answer to her question, and she was not going to be impressed by being lied to. "No," he admitted. "Art was never really my thing. I played sports and stuff like that."

Thorne took an appraising glance at her companion's physique. "You look like you played sports when you were younger."

Raine wanted to take it as a compliment, but couldn't quite get past the 'when you were younger' part. He reflexively sucked in his gut, then felt silly for doing so. He hoped she hadn't noticed.

"Allow me to teach you a few things," Thorne continued.

Raine liked the sound of that.

"Let's start with the architecture of the gallery itself," Thorne said. "Although it appears to be nothing more than a large open space with random smaller rooms tucked behind oddly placed walls, every bit of the space in a gallery is designed to enhance the experience and lead the viewer through the exhibition."

Raine glanced at his surroundings, but couldn't see the maze for the walls. "If you say so, but to me it seems like the walls are covered in so much art that I can barely notice any one painting because of all of the others. It's overwhelming, not inviting."

Thorne stopped and smiled at him. She was a tall woman, and in heels, so she didn't have to look up much to meet his gaze. Raine liked that.

"A very astute observation, Daniel," she said. "Ordinarily, each wall would have only a few items on it. Maybe even just one. The exact location of each work, and its proximity to other works that would enhance it, would be carefully decided. Perhaps even agonizingly so. But that is not, unfortunately, the case for our exhibition tonight."

"Why not?" Raine inquired.

"Because tonight is not about using the space to convince someone to purchase a single painting with a price tag in excess of a luxury car," Thorne answered. "Tonight is about giving struggling art students a fleeting glimpse of what it might feel like to have one of their pieces showcased for a wealthy buyer willing to pay a year's worth of living expenses in one transaction."

Raine glanced around again. Thorne had led them through the crowd with relative ease. Everyone had been moving out of her way. They were all her students.

"So no one is going to buy any of these?" Raine questioned. "That seems unfortunate."

Thorne shrugged. "It's possible a few will sell at the end of the evening. If any of the patrons express a real interest in a piece, then it will be part of the auction at the end of the evening. There may be a dozen or so that earn that honor, but most of them won't make it to the auction. I'm afraid most of these works will go home with their artists at the end of the evening. Richer for the experience only."

They had reached an entrance to one of those smaller side rooms Thorne had mentioned earlier. "Come inside here," she directed. "Sometimes a room like this will be used to showcase several works from a featured artist."

"And tonight?" Raine inquired.

"Tonight," Thorne shrugged, "it's for the works that didn't quite make the cut for the main room."

"Not everyone gets to be in the main room, huh?" Raine supposed that made sense.

"Not everyone got to be in the gallery," Thorne replied out of the corner of her mouth, before throwing her arms wide at the two young women within the side room. They were the only people there. "Veronica! Hailey! You made it. I'm so happy to see you here tonight!"

Veronica and Hailey looked less happy, Raine thought.

One of the women's eyes were wide, the other's were red-rimmed and glistening. Raine and Thorne had obviously walked in on something.

Thorne walked up to the red-eyed woman and took a hold of her upper arms. "Hailey, I know this is difficult for you, but it was right for you to come here tonight."

That meant the wide-eyed woman was Veronica. She was staring at Raine. He nodded awkwardly at her. "Hello."

Veronica didn't reply. She was young, early 20s, Raine estimated, with thick black hair in a simple cut and dressed in a comfortable outfit. Neither she nor Hailey, who was the same age with brown hair pulled into a ponytail, seemed to have dressed up for the event.

"We were just..." Veronica started to explain to Thorne, but faltered at the words. "I don't know. We were just talking."

"Of course," Thorne replied smoothly. She glanced back at Raine. "This is Daniel Raine. He's one of the patrons who's come to the show tonight. Daniel, this is Veronica Kwon and Hailey Parker, two of our promising young students at Cascadia."

Raine was pleased to meet a couple of the artists, but he wasn't comfortable with the label of 'patron.' He certainly wasn't going to be buying any art that night. In fact, he was starting to wonder why he'd come at all. The awkwardness in the room was palpable. He made the mistake of trying to fill it with conversation.

"Is this your work?" he tried, gesturing at the paintings on the nearest wall.

Parker clenched her jaw and looked away. Kwon's shoulders dropped.

Was it something he said?

"They're mine," Kwon admitted.

"Hailey's work wasn't quite ready for the exhibition," Thorne explained, with a hand still on Parker's shoulder.

"That's not—" Kwon began to protest. "I wouldn't say that," she amended.

They had definitely walked in on something. Raine just wanted to walk out again. He jabbed a thumb at the exit. "I think maybe I'll see if I can find Rebecca. Let you artistic types talk about, um, art or whatever."

Raine had expected Thorne to protest. Or maybe he just wanted her to. But she simply nodded. "That's probably a good idea, Daniel. It was nice to meet you. Perhaps we'll meet again."

Raine hoped so, but he was beginning to doubt it. They definitely traveled in different circles, and she didn't seem to be in any immediate need of legal services. He took his leave and dove back into the crowd in the main room of the gallery. No one was getting out of his way. He pushed through the crowd looking for the platinum hair of his sponsor for the evening. Sommers had told him he might meet some potential new clients. He doubted a couple of twenty-something starving artists were likely to be able to hire him for anything. Maybe that Caleb guy was getting divorced or going bankrupt or something else terrible that required the services of a lawyer.

He finally found Sommers near the open bar. A fortuitous location, he decided. He procured an Old Fashioned, then stepped up to his partner again.

"What happened to Selina?" Rebecca asked. "Did she spurn your advances already? I thought it would take longer."

Raine sneered at the joke. "I'll have you know that I was the one who left her company."

"Really?" Sommers raised an eyebrow at him. "You seemed to fancy her."

"It got awkward when we walked in on a couple of her students crying," Raine explained. "I'm not great with that sort of thing."

"You mean emotions?" Sommers rolled her eyes. "Typical. What were they crying about?"

Raine shrugged. "I'm not sure. I left. But Selina said something about one of them not getting her work into the exhibition tonight, so maybe something about that."

"Oh wow," Sommers responded. "That would be terrible. I'm surprised she would even come."

"Selina seemed surprised, too," Raine answered, "but supportive. She told her it was good she came."

He raised his glass and pointed at the art on the nearest wall. "Honestly, some of this stuff is pretty weird. I mean, I'm sure talent is involved, but it's not Rembrandt, you know? I wonder how bad Hailey's art had to be to get excluded from the rest of this stuff."

"Hailey?" Sommers questioned.

"That was her name," Raine explained. "Her friend's name was Veronica."

"Nice attention to detail," Sommers admired.

"Well, I'm a lawyer," Raine replied. "Speaking of which, any of your rich friends getting sued or anything else terrible? I'd love to make some money helping them."

IN THE EVENT, there was no one in immediate need of the services of an attorney, but Raine made the rounds and managed to hand out a couple of dozen business cards. Hopefully, someone would get seriously injured or discover their spouse was cheating on them or something. In the meantime, Raine would have to satisfy himself with one last non-alcoholic drink before driving back to his own post-divorce pad. At least he had upgraded from his initial studio apartment to a two-bedroom condo with a peekaboo view of Mount Rainier.

"Thanks for inviting me," he said to Sommers. He'd stayed close to her side for most of the rest of the evening. Thorne had disappeared completely, it seemed, and he hadn't found anyone else engaging enough to follow around. "It was interesting."

Sommers nodded. "Be patient. It'll be profitable too. No one is going to tell you their problems in a crowd like this. But don't be surprised if you get some phone calls tomorrow once everyone gets a moment alone again."

"Misery loves privacy," Raine quipped. But he knew she was right. If he hadn't thought so, he would have spent the evening on his couch instead of mingling with glitterati at The Finch Art Gallery. "And speaking of privacy, I'm going to hit the little lawyer's room before the auction starts. Did Duncan say how many paintings made the cut?"

Sommers grimaced. "Only eight. But if they sell for high enough, Duncan might still turn a profit."

"Knock on wood," Raine answered, but then was unable to find any within striking distance. He shrugged and returned his thoughts to his stated mission. "I'll be right back."

Sommers granted him leave, and Raine made his way

through the gathering crowd to the public restrooms in the far corner of the gallery. So far, the gala had been a dry affair. The auction was the only thing that might provide the evening with any excitement, he supposed.

He supposed wrong.

A gunshot shattered the air. It came from the women's restroom.

Without thinking, Raine dashed inside. But it was too late.

Hailey Parker was dead.

2

Hailey Parker lay on the floor of the women's restroom, her face toward the ceiling, her eyes wide and lifeless. A pool of blood was still expanding from underneath her body, soaking her hair and covering the floor one tile at a time. A bloody gunshot wound stained the front of her shirt, just over her heart. A small caliber handgun lay on the ground next to her body. The acrid smell of gunpowder and blood hung in the air.

Raine heard the sound of others on their way down the hall, but he heard a more important sound: the gallery's back door slam shut. He knew there was only one person who would be running away from the scene, rather than toward it. He bolted after the sound, dashing across the hall, through a small prep kitchen, and out into the alley behind the gallery.

The rain had picked up, filling the uneven pavement with puddles, but it also gave noise to the hurried footfalls at the far end of the alleyway. Raine sprinted into the night, chasing the splashing sound of the killer's retreat. He

ignored the sight of homeless men asleep in the other businesses' doorways, and the smell of the urine and filth mixed
with the rainwater kicked up by the two people running
through the liquid. One running away; the other running
after. Raine squinted against the rain cutting at his face,
hoping to catch a glimpse of whoever was making the
sounds he was chasing. But it was too dark, and they were
too far ahead. He ran faster.

At the end of the alley, Raine came out onto a far better
lit main street. To the right was the hill that led to the freeway. To the left, the road sloped down toward the waterfront.
He hesitated, unsure which way his quarry had run. He
knew that hesitation added to his deficit. The person he was
chasing hadn't hesitated at the intersection. They had run as
fast as they could out of that alley and turned one way or the
other. The fastest way, probably. Downhill. Raine turned left
and sprinted toward the water.

His footfalls were just as loud against the wet pavement,
but they were muffled by the sound of cars and other people
that had been absent in the alley. It was a Tuesday night, so
there weren't as many people milling about between the
nearby restaurants and bars, but the streets weren't empty
either, despite the rain.

He reached First Avenue but had to pull up short. The
walk sign was red and the light was green for the crossing
traffic. Judging by how the traffic on First was just starting to
pick up speed, Raine guessed the person he was pursuing
had made the walk signal and crossed the street without
delay. They were getting away. Every second Raine stood on
the curb was another second farther behind. He jumped into
a larger gap between two cars in the nearest lane, then
weaved his way through the next two lanes, holding up a

hand at the traffic he was impeding as if that would stop the horns and profanities, or protect him from a driver who didn't notice, or care, about his presence in the middle of a rain-darkened road.

Raine made it to the other side unscathed, and began sprinting down the sidewalk toward Western Avenue, but he was again faced with a dilemma as he tried to guess where to go when he reached that intersection. Retreating footsteps were too far away to hear anymore, and the sidewalks were too crowded to see someone running away. In fact, if the person who had bolted out of the gallery had simply pulled up into a leisurely gait next to some group of people making their way through the rain from their last bar to their next one, Raine would never have been able to tell. And he wasn't as young as he used to be. The adrenaline of the chase was wearing off and he was becoming increasingly aware of the burning in his lungs. His sprint slowed to a run, then to a jog, then to a walk. Finally, he stopped, just short of Western Avenue. Ahead, he could see Alaskan Way through the rain, and beyond it Elliott Bay. What he couldn't see, in any direction, was any sign of the person who'd murdered Hailey Parker.

"Damn it," he hissed to himself.

A few nearby people were looking at him, likely wondering why he wasn't wearing a coat, but most people ignored just another Seattleite in the rain. He pushed his wet hair away from his face and took one more futile scan of the area. Then he turned to trudge back to Finch's gallery. He could already hear the police sirens on their way.

The police cars beat him there. When he arrived, soaking wet and only just getting his breath back, a pair of patrol officers were standing out front. Raine knew they were getting ready to set up a perimeter and close off the crime scene, although they didn't have their yellow crime scene tape out quite yet. Raine expected one or both of them to yell at him to stop as he approached the front of the gallery, but they must not have noticed him. That was fine with Raine. He knew he was going to have to give a statement to the lead detective. He didn't want to explain himself more than once.

The gallery door was standing open. Raine stepped inside to a scene considerably less chaotic than he had expected. The gallery was mostly empty. He was surprised by that, if only because homicide detectives usually held every possible witness until each and every one of them had filled out a written statement, even if all it said was, 'I didn't see anything.'

Raine spied Selina Thorne and some others huddled at the far side of the gallery, but that wasn't where the action was. He stomped wet footprints across Finch's hardwood floor toward the bathroom with Hailey Parker's body. When he turned the corner into the hallway, he almost ran head-on into Sommers.

"Dan! Where have you been?" She took a moment to regard the man dripping in front of her. "Did you go for a walk?"

"I chased the murderer," Raine explained, pushing his drenched hair back from his face again.

"Murderer?" Sommers cocked her head at him. "It was a suicide."

Raine's jaw dropped open. That made no sense.

"Su—Suicide?" he managed to ask after a moment. "Is that supposed to be some kind of joke?"

"No, of course not," Sommers answered. "That wouldn't be very funny."

Raine didn't know what to say. A cold drop of water ran down the side of his nose.

"Don't take my word for it," Sommers added. She motioned to the hallway behind her. "Ask the detective. She was the one who said it was suicide."

Raine hurried past Sommers, in search of the detective, his wet shoes squeaking with each agitated step. He had just chased the murderer through the streets, albeit unsuccessfully. How could the detective conclude it was a suicide? She died of a gunshot wound to the chest.

There was no crowd at the entrance of the bathroom. Just a couple more uniformed officers. And the detective. Raine suddenly understood how the police could conclude it was a suicide so quickly.

"Detective Crenshaw," Raine practically spat the name.

Crenshaw looked over from her conversation with the gallery owner and show organizer. She frowned at him. "Do I know you?"

"We've met," Raine responded. And he hadn't been impressed. "I'm Daniel Raine, attorney at law."

"Why are you so wet?" Crenshaw followed up.

"I chased the murderer after they fled out the back door."

Crenshaw looked back toward the bathroom. Raine could see the edge of the pool of blood through the doorway. "This appears to be a suicide, Mr. Raine."

Raine ran frustrated hands through his wet hair. "Suicide? How could it be a suicide? Someone shot her in the chest!"

"Yes," Crenshaw agreed. "She did."

"She shot herself in the chest?" Raine was incredulous.

"In the heart," Crenshaw specified. "It's actually a common method of suicide. Well, maybe not common, but not unheard of either. Especially with women. Men almost always shoot themselves in the head. Women do that too sometimes, but they also shoot themselves through the heart."

Raine took a moment. "Why? Why would that be?"

"It's going to sound sexist," Crenshaw qualified, "but a medical examiner told me once that women don't want to damage their faces. Even in death, women care about being pretty."

"That is sexist," Sommers commented as she walked up behind Raine to join the conversation. "And stupid. I bet the reason women don't shoot themselves in the head is because if you mess up a shot to the heart and live, you'll just have a nasty scar, but if you shoot yourself in the head and survive, you'll be brain-damaged and permanently disabled. Women always think ahead and plan for every possible result."

Raine considered. That did seem to be a far more plausible explanation.

"Especially with a .22," Sommers added with a nod toward the bathroom. "Those will barely penetrate the skull in the first place."

"You know about firearm calibers?" Raine was surprised.

Sommers crossed her arms. "Now, that sounds sexist."

Raine supposed she was right. But they were getting off topic. "So, wait." He pointed at Crenshaw. "You're telling me that some twenty-year-old art student suddenly became despondent at her own art show, and happened to have snuck in a small-caliber handgun in her purse, and decided to shoot herself in the heart in the bathroom with a hundred people just outside?"

"Her work wasn't in the art show," Sommers said. "Selina told me it wasn't good enough."

"And that's supposed to be a motive?" Raine demanded.

"Is it even called a motive if it's suicide?" Sommers questioned. "I think it's just a reason."

Crenshaw nodded. "We only use the word 'motive' for crimes."

"Like murder!" Raine threw his hands wide. He pointed at the prep kitchen and the back door beyond. "So, what? I just imagined the killer running into the alley?"

"Did you actually see someone?" Sommers asked, hopefully.

Crenshaw looked at Raine expectantly.

"Well, no," he admitted. "But I heard them."

"What did you hear?" Crenshaw asked.

Raine felt a rush of heat up the back of his neck. Had he been mistaken?

"I heard the back door slam shut," he recounted. "And I figured the only person who would be running away was the killer."

"That would make sense," Crenshaw allowed, "if the killer weren't already dead by her own hand."

Raine shook his head. "I heard footsteps. I ran after them. I chased them through the alley and all the way down to Western."

"But you didn't actually see anyone?" Crenshaw repeated.

"No," Raine admitted. "I never saw anyone. But I could have sworn—"

"It's okay, Dan." Sommers put a hand on his shoulder. "You were trying to do the right thing. And you were very brave."

Raine appreciated the compliment, but he also felt like a child being humored.

He raised his hands to his face. "I don't know now. I just..." He pulled his hands away again and shook his head. "Suicide? Really?"

Crenshaw nodded. "Really."

Raine wasn't convinced. But he didn't want to argue anymore either. "Less paperwork for a suicide, I suppose."

"Oh God, yes!" Crenshaw almost shouted. "I mean, yes. Yes, less paperwork. No witness interviews, no search warrants, no police reports to the prosecutor's office. And I don't have to spend time looking for a suspect."

"Still an autopsy, though, right?" Raine asked.

"Yeah," Crenshaw practically sighed. "But that's just a formality at this point."

Raine grabbed that 'at this point' and put it in his pocket.

"We should go," Sommers suggested. "There's nothing more we can do here."

Raine supposed that was true.

"We'll take it from here," Crenshaw called out as Raine and Sommers turned toward the main hall.

Raine didn't bother acknowledging the comment. Sommers gave him something else to think about anyway.

"Well, tonight was a disaster," she said. "Do you think there's any way we can salvage the auction?"

"You want to hold an auction with a dead body in the women's room?" Raine questioned.

"We could make the men's room unisex for the night," Sommers replied. "There's always a solution, if you think hard enough."

"I can't tell if you're joking," Raine said.

Sommers grinned at him. "Of course I'm joking. But I'm glad you can't tell. That keeps me one up on you."

"Is there some sort of competition going on?" Raine asked.

Sommers smiled. "Always, Dan. Always."

When they reached the main hall of the gallery, the only people left in the entire building were Finch, Marquardt, and Thorne, still at the far side of the room. Raine allowed himself to be glad that Thorne had remained, but then felt guilty for feeling so, given the circumstances.

"What did the police say?" Thorne stood up and stepped over when they approached. She seemed deflated somehow. Her hair had lost its bounce. Still, Raine appreciated her proximity.

"They said they would handle it from here," he answered.

"And that we should leave," Sommers added. "Nothing like a suicide to put a damper on festivities."

"Did they say for sure it was a suicide, then?" Thorne asked.

Raine shrugged. "The detective seemed eager to accept that. If they find any evidence to the contrary, I'm sure they'll follow up on it," he said, before adding under his breath, "if they bother to look for it."

"Well, I hope it's a suicide!" Finch called out. "The only thing worse than a suicide would be a murder."

"Who would want to murder an art student?" Marquardt questioned. "That just doesn't make any sense."

Raine rubbed the back of his wet neck. The others seemed to be expecting an answer from him. "Death doesn't always make sense. Especially something like this. Either way, it's tragic, and either way, we should leave."

He was about to ask Thorne if she needed a ride home, but he stopped himself. Instead, he said his goodbyes with a round of firm handshakes. "It was nice to meet you, Mr. Finch. Mr. Marquardt. Ms. Thorne."

He pretended not to notice how warm Thorne's hand was.

"Rebecca," he nodded toward her, "thank you for the invitation. Let's not do anything like this ever again."

Sommers smiled at the joke. "Good idea, Dan. Here's hoping this is the last we hear of this terrible evening."

3

Despite his opinion of her, Raine expected to receive at least a phone call from Detective Crenshaw about what he had seen and done the night of Hailey Parker's death, suicide or not. But two weeks later, there was no word from her and Raine had, if not exactly forgotten about the bloody scene he witnessed, at least allowed himself to be distracted from the memory with the day-to-day monotony of running a law practice and figuring out what to eat for dinner every night.

It would be Rebecca Sommers who reminded him of that fateful evening. Sommers and Duncan Finch, both of whom suddenly appeared in the lobby of his office at the end of the day on a random Wednesday two weeks after the failed gala.

Raine was at the receptionist's desk, engaging in the daily small talk required among coworkers, especially when he and the receptionist, Laura Johnston, were the only employees. They weren't talking about anything important. It was just important that they talk sometimes, so they didn't spend eight hours a day ignoring each other. When the bell on the back of the front door chimed, Raine turned to see first Sommers, then Finch shrinking behind her, a shaking shadow to her statuesque figure.

"Dan," she announced, "Duncan needs your help."

Raine offered a warm smile. "I think I mentioned," he said, "I'm no art critic. I bought our office décor at Ikea."

Sommers took a moment to glance at the walls, then shook her head and pulled Finch forward to stand sheepishly next to her. "No. Duncan is being sued," she explained, "by the dead girl's family."

"Oh," Raine replied, if only to buy himself a moment to process the unexpected information.

While he hadn't expected Hailey Parker's parents to sue the gallery and its owner, he wasn't surprised by it either. It was America, after all. Land of the free and home of the lawyers. He could admire the ingenuity of it. He could even be disappointed that he hadn't thought of it first—although Sommers would likely not have taken kindly to him filing a suit against her friend. But as things landed, he could still profit from the situation, and more securely so. The Parkers' lawyers, whoever they were, would need to win a judgment at trial to earn their contingency fee. But defending a lawsuit, Raine could charge Finch by the hour, regardless of the outcome.

"Let's go back to my office." He stepped over and placed a hand on Finch's back. "Laura, could you put on a pot of coffee, please? This might take a while."

At $400/hour, plus expenses.

Finch, Raine, and Sommers made their way to the small conference room around the corner from the lobby. It was larger than Raine's personal office. They wouldn't feel so cramped. Also, Raine had left papers and what was left of his half-eaten lunch on his desk. That wasn't a good impression for a new client, even one brought to him by his part-time private investigator, Rebecca Sommers.

"Let's start at the beginning," Raine said once they had taken their seats around the conference table. "What makes you think the family of the dead woman is going to sue you?"

Finch, whose eyes were wide and didn't appear to have blinked since he'd arrived at Raine's office, reached into his jacket and extracted some papers, folded once lengthwise to accommodate the width of his coat pocket. "This. They've already filed the lawsuit against me."

Raine doubted that, even as he accepted the wrinkled papers from Finch. It was very definitely a draft of a summons and complaint, the pleadings used to initiate a civil suit. The parties were also clearly laid out on the left side of the caption:

Mark and Susan Parker, Plaintiffs, versus Duncan Finch and The Finch Art Gallery, P.S., Defendants.

And the basis for the suit was also laid out: an assertion that Finch's actions led Hailey Parker to commit suicide. But there was one thing Finch hadn't realized, either because he wasn't a lawyer, or because he was scared witless.

"They haven't filed this yet," Raine advised.

Finch displayed a frown that somehow combined relief with doubt. "How can you tell?"

Raine pointed to the caption where there was a blank space after the notation 'Case No.' "There's no case number. The clerk of the court assigns that when the case is filed."

"Why would they serve me with this if they aren't actually suing me?" That frown of Finch's turned to confusion. He looked to Sommers. "That doesn't make any sense."

"It does make sense, actually," Raine answered. "There are time limits that start ticking once you file a case. The statute of limitations on a case like this is three years, which means they could sit on it and wait three years to gather evidence and build a case before filing it. But once it's filed, then it's only a matter of months until it goes in front of a jury, and those months will be filled with motions and depositions and all sorts of things that cost money, except the lawyers don't get paid until and unless they collect at trial. It's a lot easier to scare you into thinking you're being sued and hope you'll cut them a check to avoid ever having to go to court."

Finch looked again to Sommers. "Wow."

Sommers nodded at Raine. "I told you he would know what to do."

"Was there a letter that came with those pleadings?" Raine asked, but mostly to himself, since he was the one holding the papers. He thumbed through until he found it at the back of the pages. "Aha, yes, here it is." He held it up for the others to see. "This is called a demand letter. It's really more of a threat letter. Give us so much money within ten days or we will proceed with the case that we haven't actually filed yet, and attached are the pleadings that make it look like we have sued you when actually we haven't yet. It's meant to scare you."

"It worked," Finch gasped. "So, I'm safe? I'm not going to get sued?"

"Oh no, you're definitely going to get sued," Raine answered, to Finch's obvious dismay. "They're claiming that you drove their daughter to suicide by not including her art in the exhibition. But being sued is better than just giving them what they want without a fight. Unless you want to cut a check for," he scanned the demand letter for the number, "eleven million dollars."

"I don't have eleven million dollars!" Finch exclaimed.

Raine shrugged. "You might be surprised. Does the gallery have insurance? Do you own the building? Rebecca, how much do you think that space is worth in today's commercial real estate market?"

Sommers took a moment to consider. "It's not worth that much," she appraised. "There's always room to negotiate, but even I couldn't get eleven million for it. Maybe they'd take seven million."

"Whose side are you on?" Finch snapped at her.

"Let's call selling your gallery to give them eleven million dollars Plan B," Raine suggested.

"What's Plan A?" Finch asked.

"Telling them to go fuck themselves," Raine answered, "and fighting like hell to save you and your gallery from bankruptcy for something that wasn't your fault."

Finch nodded. "I like Plan A better."

Raine grinned. "I thought you might."

"But who are their lawyers?" Sommers pointed at the demand letter in Raine's hand. "Do you know them? Are they any good?"

Raine looked again at the names on the letterhead at the top of the page, and the one under the signature at the bottom. "Amanda Stone of Churchill, Walmer, and Pickwick." He nodded. "Yeah, I know her. Well, I know of her. She's good. We'll have our work cut out for ourselves."

"What work?" Finch threw his hands into the air. "This

entire thing is ridiculous! It's going to get thrown out of court right away, isn't it?"

Raine took a long moment and a deep breath before responding. "Well, the thing is," he said finally, "the judges who decide what gets thrown out and what doesn't all used to be lawyers, and lawyers make their money by suing each other's clients. There's a lot of economic pressure to allow pretty much any lawsuit."

Finch's expression dropped. "Are you kidding me?"

Raine was not. "Let me give you an example. There used to be a doctrine called 'contributory negligence.' Basically, it meant you couldn't sue someone for damages if you were also partially at fault for them. But then some enterprising lawyer came up with the idea of 'comparative negligence.' That means if you were twenty-five percent at fault, then you could sue the other person for seventy-five percent of your damages. At first they capped it and said you couldn't sue if you were more than fifty percent at fault, but that gave way pretty quickly and now if you're ninety-nine percent at fault, you can still sue the other guy for one percent of your damages."

"That's ludicrous," Finch declared.

"Yes, but it's also the law. Now, this case." Raine held up the papers again. "You're going to be sued for something called infliction of emotional distress. It used to be that there had to be actual physical damages. Broken bones, medical bills, a smashed-up car, things like that. But then you started being able to sue for emotional damages if they were intentional. If you wage a coordinated campaign to terrorize someone, they can sue you. But again, once the foot gets in the door, the door is going to open. Lawyers started pushing to be able to sue for even the negligent infliction of emotional distress."

"Accidentally hurting someone else's feelings?" Sommers scoffed.

"Pretty much," Raine admitted. "At first there was an effort to limit it to only the intentional infliction of emotional distress. Here in Washington, they split the difference and said it had to be reckless. Reckless is halfway between intentional and negligent. It means you knew there was a risk something bad would happen, but you disregarded the risk. If they can show that, then you're going to lose."

"How could I possibly have known Hailey Parker was going to commit suicide?" Finch protested.

"You don't have to know it was going to happen," Raine explained. "You just have to know there was a risk it could have happened, and didn't care."

"But I didn't know that," Finch insisted.

"And they say you did," Raine replied. "So, the jury will decide."

"Jury!" Finch called out. "There's going to be a trial?"

Raine looked again at the demand letter and proposed complaint. "Yes. Which means we better start preparing to win it."

It was a strong statement, half trial lawyer, half salesman. "But I need to ask you a question first. It wasn't actually your fault, was it?"

Finch's eyes somehow got even wider. "Of course not! How could it possibly be my fault that that poor woman killed herself in my gallery? If anything, I'm a victim too. Do you have any idea what this sort of negative publicity is going to do to my business? I might have to sell the gallery after all and start over someplace new."

"Oh yeah, I forgot about the dead body thing," Sommers interjected. "I might not be able to get seven million if the buyers know about the dead body."

"See?" Finch pointed at Sommers. "I'm a victim. Maybe I should sue them."

Raine shook his head. "I don't think it's a good idea to sue the parents of a woman who committed suicide in your place of business."

Laura arrived then with a tray of coffee, a fresh pot and three mugs. Raine thanked her as she set it in the center of the conference table. She departed and Raine began pouring the coffee for his guests. Once everyone had a cup in front of them, Raine got down to business. "So, did you really exclude Hailey's work from the show?"

Finch frowned. "Well, yes," he admitted. "But I was just doing what I was told."

"By whom?" Raine asked. If there was someone else to blame maybe Finch would only have to pay 5.5 million.

"Selina," Finch answered.

Raine was glad to hear that, but for all the wrong reasons. Or at least some of the wrong reasons. "Selina?" he repeated.

"Yes," Finch confirmed. "I'm not sure why she wanted to exclude Hailey's paintings in particular when everyone else's art made it in. Frankly, most of the work was awful. I doubt any of it would have been good enough to hang in my gallery under normal circumstances. So I really didn't care which pieces were selected. One terrible painting was the same as any other terrible painting. I just did what she said."

Raine frowned slightly. Personally, he didn't want to pin

the blame on Thorne. Professionally, he knew the best thing he could do to insulate his client from liability was to find some other actor responsible for the damages. Thorne was an obvious target. But there was another avenue as well. Maybe his run in the rain hadn't been for naught after all.

"Our best play is to put the blame on someone else," Raine said.

"Selina?" Finch asked.

"Or Hailey herself?" Sommers suggested.

"Maybe," Raine answered, "but that's the fight they want. Make the jury choose between placing the blame on poor, desperate Hailey on the one hand or on mean old Duncan and Selina on the other. No, we need another person to blame."

"What are you getting on about?" Sommers asked, an admiring grin unfurling in the corner of her mouth.

Finch's mouth was still in panic mode. "Yes, what are you talking about?"

"We need to get Detective Crenshaw to reopen the investigation," Raine answered. "You can't be responsible for driving Hailey Parker to suicide if she was murdered."

4

R aine, Sommers, and Finch finished their consultation with Finch signing a fee agreement and agreeing to deposit ten thousand dollars into a trust account within a week, from which Raine would deduct his fees as they were earned. That was how attorneys handled defending lawsuits, at least if they wanted to be paid. Finch departed, but Raine asked Sommers to stay a bit longer.

"Am I correct to assume," Raine asked her, "that you will want to be involved in this one?"

"I am involved," Sommers answered. "Duncan is my friend. That's why I brought him to you."

"Professionally involved," Raine clarified. "I'm going to need an investigator on this case, and I'm going to bill Duncan for the investigator's time too. I just need to know if that's going to be you."

"Do you want it to be me?" Sommers asked. It didn't seem to be a challenge, or a deflection technique. She seemed to be honestly asking. So he honestly answered.

"Yes. You have insight into this art world that I just don't have. I can talk to Crenshaw by myself, but I think maybe you should be with me when I talk with Selina Thorne."

Sommers smiled. "Oh, Dan. You're adorable. You really do like her, don't you?"

But honesty only needed to go so far between business partners. "I have a job to do," he insisted.

"We have a job to do," Sommers corrected. "There's an angle I want to pursue."

Raine cocked his head at her. "What angle?"

"I'll tell you if it pans out," Sommers answered without answering. "Let me know when you're ready to talk with Selina."

Raine agreed, but the workday was over, so before he could confront Crenshaw, he was going to see the one woman who would make him forget about Selina Thorne.

"DAN!" Raine's ex-wife Natalie exclaimed when, an hour later, she opened the door to what had previously been their home. Now, it was just her home. And he was knocking on what was just her door. "You're not late."

Raine grimaced at the baggage attached to that comment. It really was the little things that killed a marriage. One person always being late. The other person never letting go of the first person always being late.

"Nice to see you again, too, Nat," Raine returned. "Are the boys ready?"

The divorce had been amicable, and the residential schedule agreed. Raine had just needed a little extra time to find more permanent lodgings. He couldn't really have their two sons over to the studio apartment he had used as almost emergency housing when he'd moved out of what he'd thought was going to be his forever family home. Now that he was settled, the schedule was week-on/week-off with a mid-week visit. One week with Raine, the next with Natalie, and Wednesday dinner with whichever parent they weren't with that week. It was the best arrangement possible, but still incredibly disruptive for the kids. Especially when they came to his condo for a week instead of sleeping in the rooms they'd had since a much younger Daniel and Natalie Raine brought them home from the hospital. Jason first, then a few years later, Jordan.

"They should be," Natalie answered without stepping aside or inviting Raine in. It was the small things. "Jordan is ready anyway."

Jordan was dealing with everything better than Jason. Raine knew from the divorce cases he'd handled profession- ally that younger kids were generally more resilient. Or at least they seemed to be at first. It was hard on everyone, but the older the kid the less able they seemed to be to adjust to the changes.

"Hi, Dad!" Jordan slipped past his mom to greet Raine. "Can we go to Olive Garden for dinner?"

Raine knew his answer was going to be yes, but he still hesitated as he considered the 30-minute drive to the nearest Olive Garden. Maybe Jason would want to go someplace closer.

"Maybe," he hedged. "Where's your brother?"

Jordan shrugged. "I dunno. He's been in his room all day."

Raine didn't like the sound of that. It wasn't the sunniest

day ever, but the rain had held off. It was a good day in Seattle to be outside at least a little bit.

"Is he okay?" Raine asked Natalie, nodding toward the interior of the house and their older son within.

"He's fine, Dan," Natalie assured him. "He's just a teenager. And he doesn't like Olive Garden."

Raine could be grateful for that at least.

"Can you go get him?" he asked his ex-wife. "Tell him the sooner he comes out, the sooner I can bring him back home."

Natalie surrendered a grimace of her own. "That may not be the motivation you think it is. But I'll see if I can get him out here."

She disappeared inside, leaving the door open enough for Raine to not be able to resist peeking inside his former residence. She had redecorated the entryway. Of course she had.

He tousled his younger son's hair. "How's school going?"

Jordan jerked his head away and fixed his hair as he shrugged. "It's school."

Raine supposed that was the honest answer.

Jason finally came outside, shoulders drooped and eyes downcast.

"Here he is," Natalie announced, walking behind him like a jail guard marching a defendant into court.

"Hey, Jace," Raine said. "How's it going?"

"Fine," Jason mumbled as he walked past everyone and made a beeline to Raine's car. Jordan hurried after him.

"I guess we're leaving," Raine said to Natalie. "I'll have them back within three hours, just like the parenting plan says."

Natalie waved it off. "We don't have to follow it to the

letter. Whatever is best for the kids. Enjoy dinner. Bring them home when you're done."

Raine appreciated Natalie's attitude. He'd done enough of those divorce cases to know there were plenty of couples who were so unable to get along that exact letter of the parenting plan was the only way to accommodate any inter-action. "Thanks, Nat," he said. Then instinctively, thinking of her not having the kids for the evening, he didn't stop himself before asking, "You have plans tonight?"

Natalie smiled at him, but it wasn't a warm smile. "You don't get to ask that anymore."

Raine knew she was right. "Sorry. I'll have them home by nine."

And he headed to his car too, looking forward to an evening with his boys, hoping they would distract him enough not to think too much about their mom, and what she was doing that night. And with whom.

5

The main headquarters for the Seattle Police Department was right downtown, at the corner of Cherry Street and Fifth Avenue, not too far from either Finch's gallery or Raine's office.

It wasn't the best day for a walk—the rain that had been threatening all morning finally materialized over the lunch hour—but after his interaction with Natalie the previous evening, Raine needed the headspace only a walk could provide; even a walk in the rain. The smell of wet pavement in his nostrils and the tingle of rain on his cheeks worked to clear his head and allow him to focus on his job and the task at hand. He just needed to keep the paper bag under his jacket so it didn't get too wet.

Raine ducked into the lobby and pushed back his hood, sending its accumulated raindrops down his back and onto the linoleum floor. The entry was spacious, but not in an inviting way. Not like Finch's gallery. It was spacious the way an empty airplane hangar might be. Large enough to suggest it held a purpose other than whatever business any small individual person might have. There were display cabinets of badges and patches on one wall, and a heroic mural to the Thin Blue Line on the other. In between was a reception desk with a single uniformed officer behind bulletproof glass. There was no one else there.

"Hello," Raine greeted the officer behind the glass after traversing the cavernous lobby that smelled of disinfectant. "Is Detective Crenshaw available?"

"Do you have an appointment?" the officer asked. He was young, early twenties at the most, with a buzz cut and cleanly shaven face. Raine guessed he was former military and had pursued one of the more common career paths for former soldiers. Raine wondered if he'd been an M.P.

"I do not," Raine admitted. "Is she here today?"

The officer frowned at him. "If you don't have an appointment, then she's not here today."

It was a clever turn of phrase, but it actually betrayed the fact that Detective Crenshaw was in fact there that day. She just wasn't taking unscheduled guests. Raine had surmised she wasn't one to add to her day's tasks, however few those might be. But everyone had to eat.

He held up the bag. "Delivery," he said. "From Mickey's."

Mickey's Diner had the best breakfasts in town. Everyone knew that. Not everyone knew they delivered. Because they didn't.

The cop narrowed his eyes at Raine. "You look a little dressed up to be a delivery driver. And a little too old."

Raine didn't think the cop needed to add that last comment, but he ignored it, for the sake of the mission. "We're all just trying to make ends meet, right? So, is Detective Crenshaw here now? Her breakfast is getting cold, and no one likes cold eggs."

"I can take it," the officer said. He slid aside a small door in the bottom of his protective partition.

But Raine held the bag back. "The instructions are that I have to hand it to her personally, in the lobby. She needs to inspect it."

"Inspect it?" The cop raised an incredulous eyebrow.

"Yeah," Raine confirmed. "Something about a citrus allergy. Although, if it's citrus, it's not actually an allergy. It's a sensitivity. But it probably feels the same when your throat swells shut. You don't want her throat to swell shut, do you?"

Of course, the officer would not want to be responsible for the death of one of his detectives. He also wasn't completely buying the 40-something-year-old delivery driver in a suit. "I'll call her."

Raine was afraid of that. But he could hardly object and stay in character. "Tell her there's extra bacon."

That did the trick, apparently. Officer Receptionist called Crenshaw, and a few minutes later Crenshaw came out to inspect her order despite never having ordered it nor, most likely, having a citrus allergy.

"Is there really extra bacon?" Crenshaw asked when she emerged from the secure door next to the receptionist kiosk.

He extended the bag to her. "Sure is. Daniel Raine. I don't know if you remember me, but—"

"Oh, I remember you," Crenshaw said without looking at him. She was looking in the bag. "You're that guy from the suicide at that art gallery. And you're a lawyer."

Raine was actually a little surprised. He didn't think she had been paying that much attention.

"You cross-examined me in court before," Crenshaw went on. "You don't forget that kind of thing. Thanks for the bacon."

"You're welcome," Raine replied. "Do you have time to talk about that alleged suicide at the art gallery?"

That made Crenshaw look up. "Alleged?"

"I still think it might have been murder," Raine told her. "I'd like to talk to you about reopening the case."

Crenshaw reached into the bag and extracted a strip of bacon. She bit off an impressively large bite and chewed it thoughtfully. When she swallowed, she smacked her lips slightly, then shook her head. "No."

"No?" Raine questioned. "Just like that? Don't you want to hear why I think you should reopen it?"

"It's not just because you don't want to feel silly for chasing a ghost through the rain?" Crenshaw ventured.

"Of course not," Raine insisted.

"I'm still not interested," Crenshaw said with a shrug. "You're a lawyer, not a cop. Your job is to do whatever your client tells you. I don't know who your client is, but I know you didn't come here just because you care about the case." Then she held up the bag. "And I know you're a liar."

"I didn't think you'd see me if I didn't have something to offer," Raine explained.

"See? Always thinking like a lawyer," Crenshaw said. "But I have to think like a cop and everything about this case points to suicide."

"What about the gun?" Raine challenged. "Who brings a gun to an art show?"

"Um, somebody who's planning on killing themselves there?" Crenshaw answered. "It's the perfect size for doing exactly that."

"Did you even try to confirm she was the one who purchased it?" Raine asked.

"It's a burner gun," Crenshaw answered. "No serial

number, no purchase records. She probably bought it at a private gun show or on some street corner downtown. Do you have any idea how many guns there are in this country? There's more guns than people. Did you know that?"

Raine did know that. "So that's it, then?"

Crenshaw though for a moment. "Yes. I'm also not going to reopen a homicide case because it helps some client of some lawyer I've met twice."

"Then reopen it because it's the right thing to do," Raine countered. "If Hailey Parker was murdered, her parents have a right to know."

Crenshaw was already chewing on another bite of bacon. "So that's who hired you? The dead girl's parents?"

"No," Raine was able to answer honestly. "Not the parents."

Crenshaw thought for a moment. "The guy who owns the gallery. What was his name? Filch?"

"Finch," Raine corrected. He didn't deny the attorney-client relationship.

"Yeah, that guy," Crenshaw confirmed. "So, what's going on? The parents are suing him? Claiming he should have prevented their daughter from killing herself, even though it was probably their fault if anyone's? That sounds like a big, fat not-my-problem."

"I would think truth and justice would be your problem," Raine grumbled.

"Come on," Crenshaw scoffed. "You're a lawyer. What do you care about truth or justice?"

Raine decided not to be offended. It would just be a waste of time, and he was hoping to salvage something of their meeting, if only to justify the cost of the meal. "Can you at least give me a copy of the autopsy report?"

"Autopsy reports are confidential," Crenshaw replied. "You can't even get those with a public records request. They're exempt."

"I know," Raine responded. "That's why I'm asking you for it. If it's conclusive, then I know there's no chance it was a murder and I can move on. But if it's equivocal, that might be important to my client's defense."

"I'm not going to tell you whether it's conclusive or equivocal," Crenshaw grumbled. "I'm telling you it's confidential."

"If you won't share the autopsy report with me," Raine tried to explain, "and I can't get it any other way, then I'll have to have my own independent autopsy conducted."

"She's been in the ground for three weeks," Crenshaw protested.

"I know." Raine nodded somberly. "We'll have to dig her up."

6

"How did your talk with Detective Crenshaw go?" Sommers asked him when next they were together. Something in her tone suggested she already knew the answer.

Raine had invited her over to his office to discuss strategy. The deadline to respond to Amanda Stone's demand letter was approaching. They were free to ignore it. It wasn't as if Finch would suddenly owe the Parkers money if he let the deadline come and go. Quite the contrary. It would require the Parkers to file an actual lawsuit, with all of the expense and pain associated with that uniquely unpleasant course of action.

But Raine wanted to be as prepared as possible when Finch came over again with that complaint for damages, only with an actual Superior Court case number stamped on it. He wanted his response to be more than just a denial of the allegations. He wanted it to be a complete counter-narrative. An alternate story of what had happened. One where Duncan Finch wasn't the bad guy. Someone else was. Raine wanted it to be The Murderer. But after his fruitless encounter with Crenshaw, he knew he needed to be open to the villain being Selina Thorne.

"About as well as I expected," Raine answered. "Actually, a little bit worse. I thought I might get a solid maybe from her, if only because that would be the easiest thing to say. And then I could work on pushing that maybe into a reluctant yes."

"It's always easiest to say no," Sommers opined. "Then you're done."

"Long term, sure. But not in the moment," Raine countered. "The very easiest is to say maybe, but mean no."

"Either way," Sommers avoided further argument on the topic, "that's a dead end."

"Maybe." Raine grinned. "But it's okay." He nodded toward his computer. "I've got a backup plan."

"Oh yeah?" Sommers asked. "What's the backup plan?"

"Uh..." Raine demurred. Somehow he wasn't quite ready to tell her he was planning on violating the dead woman's remains. "It needs a little more work. I'll show you when it's ready."

Sommers crossed her arms and frowned. "Maybe your partner could help you get it ready."

"Maybe my *investigator* could let me do the lawyer stuff," Raine returned.

"Okay, fine." Sommers uncrossed her arms and leaned back in her chair with a smile. "I'll do the investigator stuff. I've scheduled an interview with Selina Thorne."

Raine's jaw dropped, for a number of reasons.

He was surprised. "You did what?"

He was annoyed. "Without checking with me first?"

And he was excited. "When?"

"This afternoon," Sommers answered. "I know we're on a tight schedule."

Raine allowed the annoyance to take precedence. "When were you planning on telling me this?"

"Right now," Sommers answered, entirely non-plussed. She gestured at his computer. "Which is already sooner than you planned on telling me whatever your next step is."

Raine frowned at that comparison, but he decided not to argue it. Being the lawyer meant calling the shots. He didn't have to explain himself to her. But he wanted an explanation from her. Or at least details.

"When exactly are we meeting her?" he asked. "And where?"

"Three o'clock," Sommers answered. "At her office at the Cascadia Art School."

He frowned again, but only on the outside.

"You said to hit hard and hit fast," Sommers reminded him.

"I suppose I did." Raine could hardly disavow his own words. "I just thought we could hit someone else first."

"Who else?"

"Anyone else," Raine admitted.

Before he could say anything more, Laura appeared in his door frame. "Mr. Finch is here to see you," she announced.

Raine's eyebrows knitted together. He looked to Sommers. "Is this another surprise you orchestrated without me?"

"No. My plan was to meet with Duncan the day after tomorrow, after we'd spoken with Selina Thorne and Caleb Marquardt."

"Marquardt?" Raine exclaimed. "So, you have been doing even more behind my back."

"I've been doing my job," Sommers defended before adding with a grin, "behind your back."

"Should I bring Mr. Finch back?" Laura redirected them.

Raine shrugged. "Sure."

Laura nodded and disappeared to the front lobby.

"I hope it's nothing bad," Sommers worried.

Raine smiled ruefully. "I'm his lawyer. Of course it's bad."

A few moments later, Laura brought Finch to Raine's office. His cheeks were flushed and his thin chest was heaving. He held some papers in one hand.

"Mr. Finch," Laura announced, a bit unnecessarily, before retreating to her desk in the lobby.

"Duncan, what a surprise," Sommers greeted him first. "What brings you here today?"

Finch seemed a bit surprised to find anyone other than Raine in the office, but he didn't question it. Instead he simply held out the papers he'd brought. "These."

Raine took the papers from Finch.

"What is it?" Sommers asked.

"It's the same complaint," Raine answered.

"But now it has a case number," Finch added before Raine could. "That's bad, right?"

It wasn't good, Raine knew. Litigation moving forward was never good for the defendant.

But before he could say anything, Laura appeared at his office door again, papers in her hands as well. "Courier just dropped this off."

Raine took that second set of papers and compared it to the first. They were identical.

"This was delivered to us?" Raine asked Laura, just to confirm. Always confirm bad news.

"Yep. Just now."

Raine glanced at the pair of twin pleadings in his hands then looked again at Finch, who was still a bit out of breath. "Did you run here?"

The courier must have delivered Finch's copy then come straight to Raine's office.

Finch nodded sheepishly. "I was scared. I just reacted."

That was fine by Raine. What wasn't fine was Amanda Stone already knowing somehow about Raine.

"They know I'm your lawyer," he complained.

"We didn't hit fast enough," Sommers commented.

"That means we hit even harder." Raine spun his computer so Sommers could finally read the caption of the document he was drafting.

Sommers read it, then smiled broadly. "Oh, Dan. That's not just hard, that's dirty."

"What is it?" Finch asked, squinting at the screen.

"It's the first thing we're filing after our response to the complaint," Raine answered.

Sommers read from the computer screen. "Defendant's Motion to Exhume Body."

"Exhume...?" Finch gasped. "You want to dig up that dead girl?"

"Not personally," Raine answered. "Maybe not at all. But we talked about this. We need to find someone else to blame for Hailey Parker's death. The best person to blame is the person who killed her."

"She killed herself," Finch pointed out.

"Maybe." Raine was starting to like that word.

"Isn't that enough though?" Sommers challenged. "Why

do we need a murderer if we already have her as the one killing herself? Either way, it's not Duncan."

"No, the parents are alleging that Duncan caused Hailey to kill herself," Raine explained. "The best way to dispute that is to establish that she didn't kill herself at all."

"I thought you were going to talk to the cops about that," Finch said.

"They said no," Sommers answered.

Raine tapped his computer screen. "This might turn that into a maybe. I don't actually want to dig up the remains of a dead twenty-year-old. I just want everyone else to think I do."

"So, what's the timetable?" Sommers asked.

Raine considered. "I just need to put the finishing touches on this motion. The response is already prepared. I can have Laura file both of them by the end of the day."

"Good." Sommers stood up. "So, we will have time to talk with Selina Thorne."

Raine had to nod. There was time to talk with Selina Thorne, whether he wanted there to be or not. He wasn't sure which way he felt, so he surrendered to the maybe.

7

The Cascadia Art School was located north of downtown, where the eclectic Belltown neighborhood melted away into the affluent Queen Anne Hill neighborhood on one side and the parking lots and storage businesses right next to the freeway on the other. It was intersectional in that way. Vibrant and forward-looking. At least that was what the write-up on their website said. Mostly it just looked rundown and ready to be demolished for the next mixed-use office tower with a coffee shop in the lobby.

"I'd sure like to know how Amanda Stone knew Duncan hired me," Raine said as they made their way from where he had parked in one of those parking lots near Interstate-5.

"I'd like to know why Amanda Stone wants eleven million dollars," Sommers replied. "That seems like a strangely specific number."

Raine hadn't noticed that, but supposed she was right. "Huh, I don't know. Lawyers usually take a third of the recovery if a case settles, or forty percent if it goes to trial.

They probably worked backwards from what the Parkers wanted and added enough to make sure they got it after Stone took her cut."

"Is that how you do it?" Sommers asked.

"It depends on the case," Raine hedged. Lawyers always hedged. "But yeah, most of the time."

Sommers just nodded thoughtfully. Her long platinum hair was blowing in the brisk breeze.

The sky was dark in the distance. It was anyone's guess whether the rain cloud would hit Cascadia Art School, or brush past it to drench downtown or Queen Anne instead. That was life in the Pacific Northwest; dress in layers.

"So, what's the play?" Sommers asked as they approached the entrance to the art school. "Good cop, bad cop? You probably want to be the good cop, huh?"

"I'll be the good lawyer," Raine answered. "You can be the good investigator."

Sommers grinned. "I am a pretty good investigator, aren't I?"

"You're okay," Raine allowed as they reached the front door. He pulled it open.

"I'm better than okay, Dan," she said as she ducked past him into the lobby. "I think I've figured out why they're suing for eleven million."

"Wh—?" Raine started to ask he followed Sommers inside, but even that one syllable was cut short by the vision greeting them inside the Cascadia Art School. Selina Thorne stood perfectly centered in the entryway, the light from the windows at the far end of the hall illuminating her from behind, bestowing a celestial glow to her long red hair. A long floral dress flowed around her form.

"Daniel," she greeted him. "I'm so glad you came."

Raine was too.

Sommers seemed to be enjoying herself as well. She grinned at the other two, then spoke up. "Thanks for agreeing to meet with us, Selina. I know Duncan appreciates it as well."

"Oh yes, Duncan," Selina repeated the name of their mutual friend. "How is he? This must be so distressing for him."

"He's pretty distressed," Raine confirmed. He nodded toward the school behind Thorne. "Can we go to your office? This isn't really something I want to discuss where any random student might overhear us."

"Of course, of course," Thorne was quick to agree.

She turned and led them down a long corridor from the front entrance to her office, the sun still lighting her up every step of the way. The rest of the hallway was comparatively drab, with dust floating in the same beams that shined on Selina. The walls were painted a cream color with dirt smeared randomly and accumulating in the corners. The floor was uneven, with the concrete floor beneath visible through the numerous holes in the speckled linoleum. A drinking fountain halfway down the hall was missing its spigot.

The interior of Thorne's office was a pleasant contrast to the dinginess of the hallway. Stuffed guest chairs, mahogany desk, luxurious rug, overflowing bookshelves, stained glass hanging in the windows, and a collection of the most intriguing paintings filling the walls. There was a pleasant smell of something spicy but sweet. Like cinnamon, Raine thought, but not quite. Whatever it was, he liked it. He liked all of it.

For a moment, Raine forgot why they had come. When

he remembered, he wished he could forget again. As much as he enjoyed being in the company of Selina Thorne again, he had a client. And Selina stood between his client and victory. Maybe.

"Thanks for taking the time to talk with us, Ms. Thorne," Raine started as they sat in a circle of those stuffed chairs.

"Ms. Thorne?" Thorne laughed. "Please call me Selina. I know we didn't get to spend a lot of time together at the gala, but I thought we emerged friends."

Raine was heartened to hear that. "Selina," he corrected. "Thanks for meeting with us."

"Of course," she answered. "Anything I can do to help Duncan. This entire business is a tragedy. I understand that Hailey's parents are devastated, but this isn't the way to heal. At least, I wouldn't think so. I guess everyone grieves differently."

"Denial and blame are two of the stronger stages of grief," Sommers said. "I think that's what we're dealing with here."

Thorne nodded. "Of course. So, what can I do to help?"

"Help us understand the process of selecting works for the show," Raine answered, "and why Hailey's works weren't selected."

"Ah." Thorne steepled her fingers in front of her face. "Is that what they're saying? That she was despondent from not being selected for the show?"

Raine nodded. "That's their theory of the case. They're blaming Duncan for not choosing her work even though it was good enough."

"Was it?" Sommers interjected. "Was it good enough?"

Thorne blinked a few times at the question. "Well, art is very subjective."

Sommers rolled her eyes. "Of course it is," she allowed, "but some stuff just stinks, right? Some kindergartener's crayon dinosaur isn't going to be good enough to be in a gallery show. So there's some floor. Was Hailey's stuff above that floor?"

Thorne took a moment before answering. And when she did, she didn't. "Would either of you like some cardamom chai?" she asked as she stood up.

Cardamom. That was what Raine smelled.

"No, thanks," Raine answered.

Sommers passed on the chai as well. "Was Hailey's work good enough to be in the show?" she repeated. "That could be very important. If Duncan's decision to exclude it was reasonable, that could be a complete defense."

"Also, we should let you know," Raine added, "Duncan said you made the call to keep Hailey out of the show."

The sound of a spoon dropping against porcelain pierced the room. "He said what again?" Thorne asked without turning around.

"He said you were the one who decided Hailey's artwork wasn't good enough for the show," Sommers repeated. "Is that not right?"

Thorne turned around, still smiling, but no longer warmly. "I would say that is not right, no. I advocated to include all of my students in the show. It was Duncan who was concerned about the amount of available space. I told him my students would be happy to have their works resting on the floor, propped against a wall, but he insisted on maintaining what he called 'a certain level of integrity' for his gallery."

Raine looked to Sommers. She nodded. "That does sound like Duncan."

"Honestly, I don't remember the exact decision process regarding any particular student," Thorne continued. "The show was for the students, but it was still his gallery. Duncan wanted to see what was going to go up on his walls in advance, and I guess I can't blame him for that. So, I showed him digital images of every work we were considering, including several by Hailey. Our decisions were collaborative."

Raine frowned at that characterization. It still implicated his client.

"You aren't trying to blame this on me, are you?" Thorne asked. "Is that your legal strategy or whatever? Blame someone else?"

"Blaming someone else is always a potential legal strategy," Raine was quick to admit, "but no, we are not trying to pin the blame on you."

Thorne pulled herself up a bit. "Well, I should hope not." She raised a hand to her chin. "And anyway, isn't there a better person to blame than little ol' me?"

Raine was glad to hear that. And intrigued. "Who's that?"

"Why, whoever killed her, of course," Thorne replied. "What if it wasn't a suicide after all?"

Raine took a moment. "You think it might have been murder?"

Finally, someone who agreed with him.

"I know the police said it was suicide," Thorne said, "but I've been thinking about that night every day since it happened. How could you not? And the more I think about it, the less suicide makes sense."

"How do you mean?" Raine encouraged.

"She had her demons," Thorne allowed, "but we all do, don't we? That's what drives us, especially us artists. So much of the great art in the world has come from troubled souls trying to make sense of the world and their place in it. Hailey may never have become a Van Gogh, but she had a great deal of potential."

"Didn't Van Gogh kill himself?" Raine felt compelled to point out.

Thorne sighed. "Yes, so perhaps not the best example then. But the point is, she had talent. She just lacked direction. She and I had even begun having one-on-one sessions."

"Therapy sessions?" Sommers questioned.

Thorne frowned. "Not therapy. I'm not qualified for anything like that. No, just... just two artists talking about life and pain and art."

"And death?" Raine suggested. It might help his case.

Thorne hesitated. "Death is never far from the mind of a true artist. Life is fleeting. Art endures."

"It sounds like you do think she might have killed herself," Raine pointed out. "If she was spending hours obsessed with death and her legacy as an artist, only to be rejected."

"But that's what makes me think it might not have been suicide after all," Thorne tried to explain. "We talked so much about it. So deeply. So raw. She was determined to succeed despite her challenges. The more I think about it, the more convinced I am that she wasn't ready to give up."

"Which means someone else did it," Raine concluded.

"But who would want to murder some random art student?" Sommers asked.

"She was only random to those who didn't know her," Thorne replied. "To others she was a classmate, a friend—"

"A daughter," Raine knew. Then again, considering every

possible defense for his client, he felt the need to ask, "Was she any good?"

Thorne cocked her head at him. "Was she a good daughter?"

"Was she a good artist?" Raine clarified. If Duncan was right to reject her, they might not need to pursue the potential murder angle. It was dramatic, but would be difficult without the help of the police.

Thorne paused a moment before answering. "Hailey showed a lot of promise. She had some raw talent and a deep well of emotions to draw from. But she was still learning. That's why she was here. That's why all of my students are here."

She made a sweeping gesture, at the school in general, but also at the various paintings on the walls of her office.

"Did your students do these paintings?" he asked.

"Why, yes," Thorne answered.

"Are any of these paintings Hailey's?"

"Oh no, I'm afraid not," Thorne replied.

Raine stood up and crossed to one that had particularly caught his eye. It was abstract and modern. Lines and shapes and colors. He didn't know if he liked it. It made him feel both at home and ill at ease. "Who did this one?"

Thorne pushed herself out of her seat and joined Raine in front of the painting. "Well, actually, I did that one. Do you like it?"

"I do," Raine confirmed, "although I'm not sure why."

"Perfect," Thorne said. "That's exactly what I was going for."

Raine nodded to the comment, kept his eyes on the painting, and happily took in the warmth and scent of her proximity.

"Well, then." Thorne suddenly clapped her hands together and turned her attention away from the art on her walls. "Is there anything else I can help you with? I'm sorry you didn't get to enjoy any chai, but I do need to get back to my school."

Sommers looked to Raine to let him respond. He wanted to stay, but not because of the case.

"No, I don't think so," he fairly confessed.

Sommers nodded and joined the other two on her feet. "Thank you for your time, Selina."

"Of course, Rebecca," Thorne replied. "Say hi to Duncan for me. I know this must be very trying for him."

Then she turned again to give her full attention to Raine. "Thank you for coming, Daniel. I can't tell you how glad I am that one of my paintings spoke to you like that."

Raine was pretty glad about it too. But it was time to go, so he thanked her for her hospitality and then took his leave, along with Sommers. When they got outside, he turned to her. "So what do you think?"

Sommers looked sidelong at him. "I think you either need to do it or don't."

"What are you talking about?"

"Pretending to like one of her paintings isn't going to impress her," Sommers explained. "Either ask her out, or forget about her. This halfway stuff is just annoying to everyone. Especially me."

Raine frowned. Not because she was wrong. "Maybe when the case is over," he said. "Until then, Selina Thorne is nothing more than a witness."

They both knew he was lying.

He decided to change the subject. "Before we went

inside, you said you knew why they were asking for eleven million. What's your theory?"

"More like an educated guess," Sommers replied. "I ran the comps. The space for Duncan's gallery is probably worth about six and a half million dollars. And that's what's left of eleven million after the lawyers take their forty percent."

"You think the Parkers want to buy Finch's property out from under him?" Raine asked.

"I don't know if they want to," Sommers answered. "But if they win the trial, they'll be able to."

8

Raine dropped Sommers off at her office then started to navigate the maze of narrow one-way streets to his own place of business. That maze led him past The Finch Gallery and Raine felt the impulse to stop and check in with Finch. It was late, but not too late. The sun set slowly that time of year. The shadows were long, but gray, the orange of the distant sunset too weak to reach the pavement.

He pulled into a parking spot across from the front entrance of the gallery. It was marked 'LOADING AND UNLOADING ONLY.' Raine figured he was about to unload some truths on Finch. Thorne wasn't a reliable scapegoat after all. They were going to go after the potential murder angle. And that was going to be messy.

The gallery was closed already. Raine didn't know if that was normal for an art gallery, but the front door was definitely locked and the lights were definitely off. Except for some light spilling out from the backroom area. Where Hailey Parker was, one way or another, killed.

Raine considered his options. He could forget about talking with Finch, head back to his office, and work on the paper angle to the case. Or he could follow the arrow under the 'DELIVERIES AT SIDE DOOR' sign and creep around the side of the building. He chose the second option. After all, he was unloading. And he wasn't in the mood for paper.

The gallery was on a sort of corner with the main road and a narrow alleyway where the garbage bins and homeless drug addicts were kept. And deliveries were made. The dark clouds that had threatened earlier in the day had passed without releasing any rain. As a result the smell of garbage and urine, and worse, in the alley was stale. Not necessarily better than the way rain could release the stink from the pavement; just different. There appeared to be a homeless person asleep under a gray blanket a few doorways down, but he was far enough away for Raine to ignore him. Like everyone else did.

The first doorway was the side entrance to the gallery. Raine approached it and was about to knock when he noticed two things: one, a sliver of light at the crack of the not-quite-closed door, and two, voices.

"...that explanation, Finch," a man's voice was saying. "You got money for a lawyer, but you don't got the money for me?"

"I had to pay the lawyer." The whimper was definitely Finch's voice. "I could lose this place. You don't want that, do you?"

"You'll lose a lot more than just this stupid gallery if you don't come up with the money." It was a different man's voice.

There were at least two of them talking with Finch.

Raine suspected there were likely more. The strong, silent types.

"Look, look, look," Finch implored, "I can get the money. I will get the money. I'm just going to need a little more time, that's all. I didn't know that girl was going to kill herself, and I sure didn't know her parents were going to sue me."

"Maybe you should have." The first man's voice again.

"What? How could I—?" Finch whined. "You know what, fine. Sure. Okay. It's my job to make sure everything works, everything is above board. I don't want the cops snooping around here any more than you do. I'm just doing what I need to do to keep this place going so we can preserve our mutually beneficial relationship."

There was silence for several moments, then the first man spoke again. He seemed like the leader. "I'm gonna get my money?"

"Yes, yes," Finch assured him, his voice cracking.

"You just need some more time?"

"Right," Finch agreed. "Just a little more time."

"A week?"

"Uh..." Finch hesitated. "I was hoping a month."

"A month?" the first man repeated. "You hear that, Mike? He wants a month."

"A month is a long time," Mike replied.

"That's a long time, Finch," the first man told him.

"It's not that long," Finch insisted. "Three weeks. Give me three weeks."

"Oh, I'm gonna give you the whole month, Finch," the first man reassured him.

"You are?" Finch practically sobbed.

"Yeah," the man answered. "But you're gonna give me something."

Finch paused before responding. "I am?"

"Yeah," the man confirmed. "Give me your hand."

"Wh—what?" Finch's voice quavered.

"Give me your hand," the man repeated. "I'm not going to say it again."

"Uh…" Another pause. "Can I give you my left hand?"

The first man said he wasn't going to ask again and it seemed he was good to his word. The next two sounds Raine heard were a grunt from the man as he presumably grabbed Finch's hand, and Finch's shriek as he did so. The next noises were the sounds of bones breaking, followed immediately by Finch's screams. A very long scream that eventually melted into sobs.

"One month, Finch," the first man said.

And Raine knew he wasn't going to say anything more. Raine darted behind the nearest garbage bin and watched as three very large men exited the side door to the gallery and marched toward the main road. Raine never saw their faces. It was dark in the alley and they didn't even look in his direction.

Raine waited for them to turn the corner, waited a few more seconds after that, then hurried back to the gallery's side door. That time it was closed, and locked.

"Duncan!" he called out, but not too loudly, as he knocked on the door. "It's Raine. Let me in."

But there was no response.

Raine pounded on the door and raised his voice. "Duncan! Duncan!"

But the door never opened.

Raine went around to the front again. The men were gone, but so was the light emanating from the back of the gallery. The interior was completely dark, and the sun had finished its descent beneath the waves to the west. Darkness had descended on the city, and on the case.

Raine pulled out his phone, but he knew Finch wouldn't answer. He wasn't sure what to do, and he hated that. He got paid to know what to do.

He called the one person who might know.

"Rebecca Sommers," she answered. "Executive Realtor."

"Rebecca, it's Dan. You should check on Duncan."

"Is everything okay?" Sommers asked. "You sound upset."

"You haven't seen me upset yet," Raine replied. "Just reach out to Duncan tonight. He might need you. Then I need both of you at my office at noon tomorrow."

"If it's so serious, shouldn't we be there first thing?" Sommers asked. "I have a showing at ten, but we could come before that."

"No." Raine shook his head in the dark. "I'm going to be busy in the morning."

"Doing what?"

"Somebody knew Duncan hired me. And I think that same person just broke Duncan's hand."

"What?"

"It's time for me to confront my opposing counsel."

9

The Law Offices of Churchill, Walmer, and Pickwick, PLLC, were located on the 34th floor of the Columbia Tower, Seattle's tallest building. Actually the offices were located on the 34th, 35th and 36th floors, but the main receptionist desk was on 34. That was where Raine went at 8:00 a.m. the next morning. He arrived just as they were unlocking the doors. He pushed his way through them.

He'd worn his best power suit and tie combination. The one he wore for the first day of jury selection. A navy suit so dark it was almost black, a crisp white shirt, and a red silk tie. He even wore his best shoes, which he had taken the time to shine the night before. A lot of being a lawyer was playing pretend. Pretending to the client that you understood every nook and cranny of the law. Pretending to the judge that you respected their less than superlative grasp of the law and professional demeanor. Pretending to the jury that your client was innocent. And pretending to the opposing lawyer that you both didn't know that you were both pretending all of that other stuff. He might have been a solo practitioner going up against a large corporate firm with three floors of offices overlooking Elliott Bay, but he'd been around a courtroom more than most of them combined. May the best, and best-dressed, lawyer win.

"I'm here to see Amanda Stone," Raine announced.

"Uh, do you have an appointment?" the rattled receptionist asked. He obviously wasn't expecting someone to barge in as soon as he started his workday. He probably hadn't even had a drink of coffee yet. He was no more than twenty, with thick black hair and thin brown-framed glasses.

"I'm here to see Amanda Stone," Raine repeated.

"Do you have an appointment?" the receptionist repeated as well.

Appointments were overrated, in Raine's estimation. They just gave people time to prepare their lies. "Tell her it's about the motion to exhume the dead body."

The receptionist's eyes widened.

"The dead body of your clients' daughter," Raine expounded.

Those wide eyes got even wider.

"I think she'll want to see me," Raine asserted. "Why don't you give her a call and see?"

The receptionist sized up the situation and apparently decided he was more likely to get rid of Raine if he called Stone and got the directive from her to see him out. To the receptionist's obvious surprise, Stone did not so instruct.

The receptionist hung up the phone and gestured toward the seats in the waiting area of the lobby. Black leather. Very nice. "Ms. Stone will be out shortly."

Raine nodded slightly to himself. So far, so good. He just

needed to stay on the offensive. The best defense was a good offense. Everyone knew that.

"Mr. Raine?" Amanda Stone called out his name as she emerged into the lobby from the offices beyond. She was dressed even more ready for trial than he was. Same color suit, but better tailored, a creme-colored silk shell underneath, with pearls on her neck, ears and wrists. Shiny brown hair hung to the top of her shoulders. "It's a pleasure to make your acquaintance, although I do wish you had called first."

"There was no time, Ms. Stone." Raine stood to shake her hand. "My hand was forced by events that transpired just last night."

If Stone knew anything about what had happened to Finch, she didn't show it. It wasn't that her expression didn't change—that would have been a giveaway in itself—but rather it changed in the way it should have if she really hadn't known. Curiosity, but not too much.

"Do tell," she replied. "Well, let's go back to my office and you can tell me all about that, and why you think any judge in this state would ever let you dig up a dead girl over the objections of her parents. Ryan, some coffee, please?"

"Right away, Ms. Stone," Ryan the Receptionist called out.

Then Stone led Raine to her office. He knew it was going to be nicer than his. And he guessed Ryan's coffee would be better than Laura's as well.

He was not disappointed. Stone's office was spacious and modern, with a view of both Elliott Bay and Mount Rainier. She didn't even need to turn the lights on, it was so well lit from the floor-to-ceiling windows. She bid him to sit in one of her leather guest chairs and sat across her desk from him in her own leather desk chair.

"J. Daniel Raine, attorney at law," Stone began with a grin. "I don't believe we've crossed paths before."

"Dan is fine, thanks," Raine replied, "and no, I don't believe so either. I guess there's more than enough misery to go around for all the lawyers in town."

"Luckily for us," Stone said. "So, why add to the misery by traumatizing my clients with the threat of digging up their dead daughter?"

Right to the point. Raine liked that.

"Why traumatize my client by suing him for something that clearly wasn't his fault?" Raine returned. "However Hailey Parker died, it wasn't caused by Duncan Finch."

"The Duncan Finch Gallery," Stone qualified. "You remember law school, don't you? They taught us to always sue the deepest pocket. Cascadia Art School is all but bankrupt, as you might expect given the nature of the endeavor. But your client has a healthy business."

"Not healthy enough to pay you eleven million dollars," Raine countered.

"He also has a very large umbrella insurance policy," Stone smirked. "You should just refer it to them, take your fees to date, and move on to the next case."

"So I don't pursue the whole body exhumation thing?" Raine knew.

"It would be nice to avoid that fight," Stone admitted. "I'll defeat the motion in court, but I would like to spare my clients the emotional turmoil of worrying about the outcome."

"You could drop the case," Raine suggested. "Then I wouldn't need to dig up the body."

"Is that it? Blackmail?" Stone laughed. "That's very basic of you. We're not going to drop our suit just because it becomes slightly uncomfortable. I'm confident I will repel your motion. No judge in this county is going to agree to dig up a dead girl based on the grounds you presented. What was it? 'The possibility of homicide'? You're going to need more than a mere possibility, especially when the police concluded it was suicide."

"I'm working that angle too," Raine assured her.

"Oh, I know that too," Stone seemed pleased to say. "Good luck with Detective Crenshaw. She is not the most motivated officer on the force. I can't see you convincing her to reopen a case she's already closed."

Raine took a moment to pause the rapid fire back and forth. "You seem to know an awful lot about my activities. How did you know Mr. Finch had even hired me?"

"We didn't get to be Seattle's most successful personal injury firm by not staying one step ahead of our opponents," Stone answered without really answering. "When we choose a target, we find out everything about that target. And their lawyers. How are Jason and Jordan adjusting to the divorce, by the way?"

That was too far. Raine raised a finger in warning at her. "Don't mention my kids."

Stone smiled at him. "See? That feeling you have right now? That's how my clients feel about you trying to desecrate their daughter's remains."

"I have a job to do," Raine defended.

"So do I," Stone replied. "And I can tell you right now that if you go forward with that motion, there is no way we will settle this case for less than what was in our demand letter."

"Now that sounds like blackmail," Raine remarked.

Stone shook her head. "That's negotiation. You drop your

quixotic motion and let's see if we can come to a settlement that gets our clients satisfied and ourselves paid."

Raine ignored the overture. "Speaking of blackmail, you wouldn't happen to know anything about my client owing money to any dangerous people, would you?"

Stone's expression shifted ever so slightly. Enough for Raine to notice. Not enough for him to draw a solid conclusion. "I'm afraid not. But I wouldn't want to be in your position, having a client who already owes other people money."

Raine fought off a frown. Stone wasn't wrong.

"Lawyers aren't cheap," Stone continued. That wry grin returned, but darker. "They can cost an arm and a leg."

Raine just stared at Stone for several seconds. It was time to leave.

He stood up. "I'll see you in court, Ms. Stone."

Stone stood up too and offered her hand. "I'll see you there as well."

Raine couldn't tell if the 'as well' referred to her also seeing him, or her seeing him also in court. Clearly someone was watching his movements. He didn't shake her hand. "I'll see myself out."

10

Finch's left hand was in a cast. Of course it was. Raine had heard it break.

He nodded at it. "You going to tell me how that happened?"

They were in Raine's office—Finch, Raine, and Sommers. It was just after noon. Raine was in no mood. He hadn't eaten yet.

"This?" Finch glanced at his broken hand. "Oh, it's nothing. I just fell awkwardly. I was on a ladder, trying to hang a new painting I got from—"

"Do. Not. Lie to me," Raine interrupted. "I heard them break your hand."

Finch's eyes darted down, over to Sommers, then back to Raine. "I-I don't—"

"I came to talk to you about what Selina told us," Raine explained. "I went to the side door. It was open a crack. I heard everything."

Finch didn't say anything.

"Well, not everything," Raine admitted. "I didn't hear

why you owed them money, but I heard them grant you a one-month extension. And I heard what you had to pay for that."

Finch held Raine's gaze for a moment, then dropped his head.

"I guess I appreciate that you paid me first," Raine offered. "I certainly am not going to injure you if you fail to pay your retainer. But I am worried about, among other things, your ability to pay me any further."

"That's what you're worried about?" Sommers chided.

"I said 'among other things'," Raine defended. He pointed at Finch's cast. "Does that have anything, anything at all, to do with our case? And you had better not lie to me."

Finch shook his head. "I swear it has nothing to do with the case. I just... I just like to gamble a little bit. I made a couple of bad bets, had a couple of bad breaks. I was going to be fine, but then those damned parents sued me and I panicked and paid you instead of those men, like I should have. And, well," he raised his hand, "this happened. At least it's a clean break."

"Oh, Duncan." Sommers grabbed him by his good arm. "You should have told me. I could have helped."

Raine wasn't convinced Finch's money troubles, and resultant physical injuries, were completely unrelated to the litigation. Stone seemed to know about it. Why would she, unless she had an interest in it. Maybe she represented the loan sharks too. He wouldn't put that past her.

He needed to know two things before he continued.

"Are you going to be able to pay me?" He wasn't going to fight Amanda Stone *pro bono*.

Finch nodded meekly. "Just like I told those men. I have resources. I just need a little time to get things more liquid."

"Are you going to lie to me again?" He wasn't going to fight Amanda Stone hamstrung by his own client.

"No," Finch answered, almost too quickly.

"Duncan." Sommers pointed a finger at him. "You can't expect Dan to win the case if you lie to him."

"No, I won't lie," Duncan repeated. "I swear."

"Let's test that," Raine said. He raised his chin at Finch. "Why did you reject Hailey Parker's artwork? And remember, we talked to Selina Thorne yesterday."

Finch took a moment before answering. Raine did not find that reassuring. Finch looked to Sommers then hung his head again. "Because it was terrible! I mean, just awful." He looked up again. "It was beyond amateurish. My eight-year-old niece could have done better with a crayon between her toes. I know it was supposed to be a charity show but even charity has its limits."

"It was your gallery after all." Raine knew. "You needed to maintain a certain level of integrity."

Finch jabbed an affirmative finger at him. "Yes. That. Exactly."

Raine frowned and looked to Sommers.

She shrugged. "At least we know he's not lying."

Raine found small comfort in that. He had hoped Selina had been the one lying. She wasn't his client.

Raine ended the meeting with Finch with two warnings: no more lying, and no missed payments. Then he dismissed his client, but asked his investigator to stay.

"This is not good," he told her once Finch had departed. "Duncan is compromised. Even if he's telling us the truth about it being a gambling debt, it makes him open to manipulation."

Sommers considered for a moment, her lips twisted into

a burgundy knot. "You're not wrong, but so what, as long as you get paid?"

Raine frowned. "I want to win too. It's not just about the money. It's about doing a good job. Reputation. It's about my reputation."

"I understand the importance of reputation," Sommers agreed. "Beating this Amanda Stone would build yours?"

Raine shrugged. "Losing to her sure won't. Especially if it's because I didn't have control of my own client. What if he goes sideways on the stand at trial? It's going to be hard enough to get around his rejection of Hailey's art. I don't need the promise of forgiven debts—"

"Or the threat of more broken bones," Sommers added.

"Exactly," Raine agreed. "I don't need that to make him change his story at the last minute and we lose the case."

"Do you think that's likely?" Sommers asked.

"I think there's more going on than we know right now," Raine answered. "Anything could happen."

Sommers nodded. "So, what's next?"

Raine surrendered a dark smile. "I'm going to dig up a dead body."

11

The hearing on Raine's motion to exhume the remains of Hailey Parker was scheduled for a Friday afternoon. Mondays through Thursdays, most of the courtrooms were busy conducting trial. On Fridays, the jurors got to go home, but the judge and the lawyers used the day to deal with all of the other, pretrial, matters that needed to be addressed before Monday rolled around again.

On the day Raine filed his response to Stone's complaint, he also filed his motion to exhume the body and the notice of hearing to argue that motion. He scheduled the hearing for two weeks after that. When they arrived that afternoon on the miscellaneous civil motions docket, there were four other hearings scheduled, but none of them was even half as interesting as his.

Raine arrived first, Finch in tow. Raine could have done the hearing without his client present, unlike in a criminal case where a defendant's presence was required at any 'crucial stage' of the proceedings. Raine had been tempted to tell

Finch to stay away. He wasn't looking forward to having an anxious ball of nerves vibrating next to him throughout the hearing. But he knew Stone was going to bring her clients, and judges were only human. They were more likely to say something bad—like an adverse ruling—about someone who wasn't present. Finch's presence wouldn't win the hearing, but his absence could lose it.

Raine led them to some seats in the front row of the courtroom, right behind the table with the nameplate on it that read, 'DEFENDANT.' Raine extracted a blank legal pad and a spare pen from his briefcase and pushed them over to Finch.

"You don't need to take notes," Raine said, "although you can if you want. But if you have any questions or concerns, I can't have you whispering in my ear while I'm trying to listen to the judge or the other lawyer. Write it down and I will look at it when I get a chance. Understood?"

Finch looked, doe-eyed, at the yellow paper, then at his lawyer. "Okay," he agreed.

Raine noticed just how deflated Finch seemed. He looked absolutely terrified and lost. Luckily, there would be no testimony. It was a purely legal argument. Speeches by the lawyers, a ruling by the judge. But Raine was going to have to work with Finch prior to the trial if he was going to convince the jury to believe anything Finch had to say to them. One more thing for the to-do list.

Stone entered then, her clients with her as Raine expected. It was Raine's first glance at his opponents. He was not pleased by it. That jury who was going to dislike Finch was going to love the Parkers. They were the picture of a nice married couple. In their fifties, graying and a little heavy, dressed respectfully but simply, expressions appropriately pained given the circumstances. They looked like they would be good neighbors, ready to loan whatever was needed and never worry about getting it back. Appearances weren't everything, but in the world of jury trials, they weren't nothing either.

Stone directed her clients to sit in the back row of the courtroom then came forward to where Raine was sitting. "Mr. Raine," she greeted him coldly.

"Ms. Stone," Raine returned the greeting, in tone as well.

"Are you certain you don't want to drop this motion before the judge comes out?" Stone suggested. "My clients would probably accept eight million. But no deals if I have to argue this motion."

"What if I win the motion?" Raine replied. "Maybe we could negotiate between that result and actually exhuming the body. I feel like that might motivate your clients to settle for a more reasonable amount."

Stone's smile gained some actual warmth. "I like that attitude, Raine. I'm glad to see you have a little fight in you. It's more fun to win that way."

Raine felt increasingly comfortable in his dislike of Amanda Stone. "Nice trash-talking with you. I'll look forward to your advocacy when the judge comes out."

Stone departed with a tight smile but no further words.

Finch started to comment on her, but Raine hushed him. The judge would be out soon. All five hearings were scheduled for 1:00 p.m. Obviously, they couldn't be argued all at once. The judge would take them one at a time, and that would fill up the afternoon until it was finally time for everyone to go home for the weekend.

Motions were assigned randomly to one of the 53 judges on the King County Superior Court bench. The judges rotated through different assignments that could last from several months to a few years. Some of them were handling criminal matters, others were at the juvenile court, while still others were presiding over family cases. The ones who remained handled the civil matters like the wrongful death suit brought in the matter of *Mark and Susan Parker, Plaintiffs, versus Duncan Finch and The Finch Art Gallery, P.S., Defendants. Parker v. Finch*, for short.

The judge hearing the civil motions that afternoon was Judge Jennifer Castro. She had been a judge for almost a decade, having won an election for an open seat after the retirement of one of the previous generation of judges. She was generally well-liked and well-respected, so no one ran against her at the next election, or the one after that. You didn't run against a sitting judge unless you expected to win. *'When you strike at a king, you must kill him.'* And no one thought they could beat Jennifer Castro in an election.

The good news was that she was a reasonable judge who cared about how her decisions impacted the litigants before her and the community outside the courthouse. That was also the bad news, at least for Raine.

"All rise!" the bailiff bellowed. "The King County Superior Court is now in session, The Honorable Jennifer Castro presiding."

Judge Castro emerged from her chambers and took her seat above the courtroom. "Please be seated," she instructed. She was in her early 50s, but like a lot of people in Seattle, she was fighting the steady progress of aging with healthy food and long hikes. She had shoulder-length black hair and wise-looking brown eyes. Everything else was hidden under her black robe.

"Do we have any matters ready?" she asked, ostensibly to her bailiff.

What she really meant was whether there were any matched pairs yet; cases where the lawyers for both sides had already arrived and checked in. Most lawyers couldn't stay in business with only one client, and Friday afternoons often featured attorneys dashing from courtroom to court-room as they handled more than one motion for more than one client. But both of the lawyers were there on the *Parker v. Finch* matter and so that was the one Judge Castro called first.

"Will the lawyers please step forward and state your appearances for the record?" she bade.

Raine and Stone both made their way to the bar, which was really a counter, below the judge bench and awkwardly close to the court-reporter and bailiff seated on the other side of the wooden shelf top.

"Amanda Stone, of Churchill, Walmer, and Pickwick," Stone began—the plaintiff always spoke first—"appearing on behalf of the plaintiffs, Mark and Susan Parker, and the estate of their daughter, Hailey Parker."

"Daniel Raine, appearing on behalf of the defendants, Duncan Finch and The Finch Gallery."

"All right, thank you," Judge Castro accepted their appearances. She turned to the motion at hand. "Now, from the briefing I've read, this is a motion to—" she held up a page of what was likely Raine's motion, "—exhume a dead body. Is that correct?"

The incredulity in the judge's voice did not enhearten Raine. "That is correct, Your Honor."

"A suicide victim," Judge Castro continued. "Is that correct?"

"Yes, Your Honor," Stone answered, although it seemed to Raine that the question had been put to him.

"Well, you see, Your Honor, that's the issue," he said. "The plaintiffs' theory of the case is that their daughter committed suicide as a proximate result of the negligent actions of my client. Setting aside for a moment whether one person can legally be held accountable for another person's suicide—"

"Oh, they can," Stone interjected. "Even in a criminal context, which has a much higher burden of proof. The State has secured convictions for manslaughter in such situations."

Raine smiled thinly at Stone, then looked up at Judge Castro. "I'm sorry, Your Honor. Is it my turn to speak, or are we all just going to yell out bids like we're at an auction?"

Judge Castro cocked her head down at Raine and offered her own slight grin. "This is no auction, Mr. Raine, I assure you." She turned to Stone long enough to ask her to wait for her turn to speak, then back to Raine. "Please continue, counsel. I believe you were saying something about setting aside the issue of causation for a moment?"

"Yes, right," Raine accepted the prompt. "Setting that aside, there is actually a more preliminary inquiry to be made. Namely, whether Ms. Parker's death was actually a suicide. If it was not, but rather was a homicide, then there can be no liability for causing a suicide that wasn't a suicide."

"Didn't the police determine it was a suicide?" Judge Castro asked.

Raine chose his next words carefully. "The detective in the case apparently did not find facts sufficient to pique her curiosity to explore options outside of the conclusion that most expeditiously closed the case."

Judge Castro smiled down again at him. "Are you saying the detective was wrong?"

"I'm saying none of us are required to accept the word of a detective," Raine answered. "If we were, then we wouldn't need half of the courtrooms in this courthouse. Every criminal defendant could simply be convicted because some police officer somewhere in the department hierarchy concluded the defendant was guilty. But we don't do that. In fact, we tell jurors that police officers are not necessarily any more credible than any other witness. Some people might even suggest police officers are less credible than other witnesses. Not me, of course, but some people.

"All I'm asking is that someone other than a police officer, or a medical examiner affiliated with the police department, be allowed to make an independent determination as to the manner of death. If this wasn't a suicide, we can save a lot of people a lot of time and trouble. Oh, and set the police on the path to finding the murderer and bringing true justice to this case."

"The police you just said you don't trust?" Judge Castro questioned.

"Some people, Your Honor," Raine replied. "I said, 'some people'."

"Mm-hm," Judge Castro replied skeptically. She turned to Raine's opponent. "What say you about all this, Ms. Stone? And by the way, it's nice to see you again."

"It's nice to see you again as well, Your Honor."

Raine stifled a grimace. Big firms like Churchill, Walmer, and Pickwick always donated to the campaigns of judges who were going to win. Solo practitioners like Raine could hardly compete in that arena.

After the coded wink-and-nod with the judge, Stone responded to her prompt. "What I say to all of this, Your Honor, is that the Court should not—nay, must not—allow the defendant to further victimize the poor, grief-stricken parents of Hailey Parker. It is bad enough that Mr. Finch's arbitrary, capricious, and negligent action in excluding Hailey from her school's preeminent art showing led directly and proximately to her decision to take her life that very night. Now, Mr. Finch, through his lawyer, is seeking to mock that tragedy. He is asking this Court to allow him almost literally to urinate on their daughter's grave."

Wow, Raine thought, *that was a strong assertion.*

"Worse than urinate, Your Honor," Stone continued. "Mr. Finch, through counsel, wants to desecrate the body of the Parkers' only daughter, and for no other reason than to torment them into dropping their claim against him. I can tell you, Your Honor, that the Parkers authorized me to try to settle this case prior to this hearing to avoid even the smallest risk that this Court might grant this truly heinous request. But Mr. Finch, through counsel, refused."

Raine felt comfortable that everyone understood 'Mr. Finch, through counsel' meant him.

"This is nothing but a fishing expedition of the worst kind, Your Honor," Stone continued.

Raine stole a glimpse at her support team in the front row; they were enraptured, leaning forward for the next word.

"Mr. Finch has presented no information to this Court to call into question the conclusions of the proper authorities in this case. He is simply trying to harass my clients by holding hostage the body of their dead daughter, a death he caused. My clients are present in court, Your Honor, and are more than ready to testify as to how this motion, if granted, would affect them. Indeed, if the motion is granted, we will have no choice but to amend our complaint to seek additional damages for the intentional infliction of emotional distress."

"Unless Mr. Raine is correct," Judge Castro cautioned, "and a second forensic examination of the body reveals evidence of a manner of death other than suicide."

"We are confident such an examination would reveal no such evidence, Your Honor," Stone replied.

"Then why not let it happen?" Castro proposed. "Legally speaking, the worst thing that happens is that both sides have additional information. That can only be a good thing, wouldn't you say?"

"Legally, perhaps, Your Honor," Stone allowed, "but there is more to what we do than the cold, black letter of the law. We don't just follow the law, Your Honor. We pursue justice. Truly, there is no higher calling than ours. And what is justice but the sum of the good and right things happening to the right people for the right reasons. People, Your Honor. Not words in some statute book or dusty old volume of Supreme Court cases. People. Your Honor cannot make this decision in a vacuum without considering the real impact it will have on real people. Real people like Mark and Susan Parker."

Stone turned around and gestured again at her clients, then turned back to conclude her appeal.

"They lost their daughter, Your Honor," Stone let her voice crack ever so slightly. Raine knew it was intentional. He knew Castro knew that too. "Their wonderful, beautiful, talented, creative, one-of-a-kind daughter. They buried their child, Your Honor. Let her stay buried. Let her well and truly rest in peace."

Castro nodded down at Stone's advocacy. Just because she knew what it was didn't mean she wouldn't be persuaded by it. She swung her gaze back to Raine. "This is your motion, Mr. Raine. You have the last word. Any reply?"

Raine took a moment, then stood. "Yes, I have a reply, Your Honor. My reply is that Mr. Finch didn't ask for this litigation. He didn't ask to be sued. All he was trying to do was help out a group of poor art students, students who might never again get to see their artwork hanging in a gallery. But as they say, no good deed goes unpunished. So, now he sits here, blamed for something someone else did, facing the very real possibility of losing everything he's worked so hard to build. The irony is stunning. A man who runs a gallery to showcase local artists loses that business for doing just that. How would that help our local art community, from the students at Cascadia Art School to the starving artists up and down Puget Sound? Do any of them benefit from Mr. Finch having to sell his gallery to pay a judgment, and that space turning into a pawn shop, or a noodle restaurant, or maybe more self-storage lockers?"

Raine gestured at his opponents. "They are the ones who filed this lawsuit. They are the ones who decide whether it proceeds forward. But if they decide to push forward, then Mr. Finch is going to push back. He will defend himself and his business to the utmost of his ability. And if the plaintiffs allege that Mr. Finch is liable for their daughter's apparent suicide, then that calls into question every aspect of their complaint, beginning with the assumption that it was a suicide in the first place. If they are going to allege that, then we get to test that allegation in every possible way. Or they can drop the lawsuit. The choice is yours."

Judge Castro had listened to Raine's speech stone-faced. Not necessarily in a bad way; judges were supposed to maintain an air of neutrality. Raine waited for the expression to break. An experienced attorney could glean a lot from whether the judge's expression broke with a nod or a frown, a sigh or a wry grin. Castro twisted her lips into a knot. That meant she thought he had a point. He waited to see if she thought that was enough.

"I appreciate Mr. Raine's argument," the judge began her ruling.

Judges never started with the actual result. It was always a lengthy explanation, during which both lawyers would alternatively think they were going to win based on one sentence, only to then think that they were going to lose based on the next sentence. Raine couldn't stop that thought process, but he had practice in turning down its volume and pushing it to the back of his mind while he waited for the judge to reach the end of her soliloquy.

"One could say that Mr. Finch is only here because a complaint was filed against him, and so the people responsible for bringing him here, the Parkers, should not be surprised that he would defend himself vigorously."

The sentence that could make Raine think he was going to win, if he allowed it.

"On the other hand," Judge Castro continued, "one could argue that Mr. Finch is here because of his own actions, and it was those actions that led the Parkers to bring the case, as is their right to do under the law. We don't blame the prosecutor for filing charges against the criminal. Why then should we blame the civil plaintiff for seeking redress for an alleged wrong against them?"

The sentence that could make Raine think he was going to lose.

"And should we allow a plaintiff to be further victimized by a defendant who has wronged them?"

An even worse sentence for Raine. But he waited for the one that mattered, the last one the judge would utter. He folded his hands and waited. A stolen glance at Stone revealed she was doing the same.

"I want both parties to know that I take this matter very seriously," Castro said. "Regardless of the outcome of the case, a young woman has died. Her parents are undoubtedly heartbroken. Our justice system is undoubtedly flawed, but it is also perhaps the greatest such system ever crafted. There are countless practitioners, judges and lawyers alike, who have dedicated their lives to its constant improvement. And yet, it has inherent limitations. Nothing I do, nothing the attorneys do, nothing the jury does can undo the core tragedy of this case. Nothing will bring Hailey Parker back."

The harsh reality of the judge's undeniable comment was punctuated by a sob escaping from Mrs. Parker. All eyes reflexively turned to her, even if only momentarily, as Stone quickly put a consoling arm around her shaking client.

"And I think it is that tragedy that ultimately sways my decision. This Court cannot undo what happened to Hailey Parker. But it can prevent anything further from happening to her."

Judge Castro looked down at the defense table. "Mr. Raine, I will sign a subpoena for the release of the autopsy report authored by the King County Medical Examiner's Office, but I will not sign an order authorizing the exhumation of Hailey Parker's remains. The defendant's motion is denied."

Finch sighed. "I'm kind of relieved," he confessed to Raine in a whisper.

Raine appreciated the sentiment. Finch was a good person. That made it easier to defend him. Which meant Raine couldn't always be a good person.

He stood up again to address the Court. "Thank you, Your Honor," he made sure to say. "If the autopsy report reveals additional information relevant to the Court's consideration of our original motion, may we renew our motion?"

Stone stood up as well. "We would object to that, Your Honor," she interjected before Castro could rule. "The defendant brought this motion. He should have and presumably did present all necessary evidence and argument, but the Court wisely denied his motion. My clients should not have to live with the constant threat of their child's remains being defiled."

That was the threat Raine wanted to keep alive. "I can hardly have presented information I don't yet possess," he pointed out.

Judge Castro decided to avoid the issue. "I have made my ruling. I will not prejudge further motions which may or may not be brought. I will only say that the bar for such a motion will be very high indeed. Do you understand, Mr. Raine?"

He did. It meant there was a chance. And he knew Stone understood that too. Raine was going to walk away with the autopsy report and still holding the bargaining chip of renewing his motion. He was going to call that a win.

12

J ust because Judge Castro signed a subpoena for Raine to get Hailey Parker's autopsy report didn't mean he was going to get it immediately. For one thing, government agencies were not known for their speed of response generally. For another, the medical examiner's office didn't particularly want to release what would otherwise be confidential information, so they weren't about to drop everything to provide the documents. "Five to ten business days," they told Raine.

He could have noted a motion for Judge Castro to amend her subpoena to provide the records immediately, but the court rules required he give at least five court days' notice to the other side. That meant it wouldn't really be any quicker, and Stone would have an opportunity to object again and ask Castro to reconsider issuing the subpoena at all. No, the better route was patience. Raine would get the report, and in the meantime, other things could develop. They always did, in his experience.

On the day the autopsy report was ready for pickup,

Raine decided to walk the few blocks from his office to the King County Administration Building, located conveniently between the King County Courthouse and the King County Jail. There were even skybridges connecting the buildings, although they were reserved for marching inmates from the jail on Fifth Avenue to the courtrooms in the courthouse on Third Avenue. The King County Medical Examiner's Office was on the third floor of the Admin Building. The morgue was off-site, which was fine with Raine. He hadn't been particularly interested in observing a new autopsy anyway, especially not on a body that had been decomposing for over a month. Hopefully the report would give him what he needed. He didn't need it to say Hailey Parker's death was a murder. He just needed it to say there was even the smallest possibility it wasn't suicide.

"Hello," Raine greeted the woman at the front desk of the M.E.'s office. "I'm attorney Daniel Raine. I believe there's some documents ready for me to pick up."

The woman frowned at him. She was about his age, somewhere in her 40s, and looked like she spent her week-ends doing cross-fit or running marathons or engaging in some other intense exercise Raine wasn't about to even consider. Although that sprint through the rain, or rather the way he'd run out of breath so quickly, made him think he needed to get to the gym a bit more often than once a year.

She grabbed a sealed manilla envelope to her left and handed it to Raine without uttering a word. It had his name on it in black marker.

"Thank you," he tried with his best smile.

No smile was returned. She was probably irritated that he got something they didn't want him to have. Such was the life of a lawyer. There was always someone upset with you about something. He raised the packet in salute and departed. "Nice talking with you."

Once in the hallway, he set to tearing the envelope open, but his phone rang. Not many people had his personal cell number, so calls were rare, and usually important. He checked to see who it was, on the off chance he needed to speak with them. On the off chance it was Natalie.

It wasn't, of course. It was Sommers. He decided to answer it.

"Hello, Rebecca."

"Hey, Dan," came his partner's voice on the other end. "You got a minute?"

"Sure," Raine answered. "What's up? Did you solve our latest case?"

"Maybe," Sommers answered.

Raine was surprised. He wasn't sure there even was a solution, per se. "Really?"

"Do you like ice cream?" Sommers asked, not at all in reply to his question.

"Ice cream?" Raine confirmed, frowning to himself. "I mean, everyone likes ice cream, right?"

"Meet me at the ice cream shop at Yesler and Occidental," Sommers instructed.

Raine looked out the window. It wasn't cold that day, but it wasn't warm either. Typical Seattle. At least it wasn't raining. "Isn't it a little cold for ice cream?"

"You just said you liked it," Sommers pointed out.

Raine wasn't sure how he'd gotten into an argument about having ice cream on a cool Seattle afternoon, but he didn't want to extend it any further. "Okay. Give me fifteen minutes. I'm at the Admin Building. I just picked up the autopsy report."

"Oh good," Sommers said. "Bring that. Then we'll have two things to talk about."

Three, Raine thought.

THE ICE CREAM shop was actually on Occidental Avenue, a few doors down from the corner with Yesler Way. It was around the block from Finch's gallery. Raine expected that was the point. Sommers was waiting outside, dressed to kill as usual, and a broad grin on her face. She already had a cone of something brown with chunks in it.

"You already ordered?" Raine complained.

"You said fifteen minutes," Sommers answered. "It's been seventeen. I'm on a schedule."

Raine didn't doubt that. Luckily, no one else seemed to share her enthusiasm for frozen treats at that particular moment and Raine was able to order a scoop of raspberry sherbet without having to wait in line.

"Come on." Sommers gestured down Occidental with her ice cream. "There's a bench we can sit on."

Raine complied, and they made their way to a bench facing the building across the street, with its four storefronts. The door the farthest to the right was The Finch Gallery, next to the alley Raine had already spent an inordinate amount of time in. The bench had bird droppings on it, of course, but there was enough clean space for the two of them to sit and look across at the scene of Hailey Parker's death and Duncan Finch's assault.

"See those businesses over there?" Sommers asked.

"Not sure how I couldn't," Raine responded. "I assume you have some information about them?"

Sommers nodded. "The one on the far left is a gym now, but it used to be a restaurant. The owners had to sell after a fire. Insurance didn't cover enough to rebuild. They had to sell it at a discount to cut their losses."

"You looked up the title record?"

"Records," Sommers corrected. She was making good progress on her ice cream. Raine had to remember to keep his from running down his hand. "Look at the next one over. It's a convenience store now, but it used to be a bookstore. They sold for under market too. The owner died unexpectedly and his widow didn't want to be left running the business alone. Too many memories."

"That sounds like more than just real estate records," Raine noted.

Sommers grinned. "I know everyone who sells real estate in this town. Most of them owe me a favor. And all of them talk."

She gestured with her cone at the third storefront, the one next to Finch's gallery. "That one has been a sandwich franchise for years now, but it's under new ownership. The previous owner overextended himself and had to declare bankruptcy. The new owner bought it out of receivership at auction."

"So, some people got some good deals on this block," Raine noted. "I'll try to keep Finch from having to sell his gallery for under market."

Sommers shook her head. "I don't think it's different people. I think it's the same person. Or at least they all use the same law firm."

Raine suddenly became more interested. "Churchill, Walmer, and Pickwick?"

"Yep." She reached into her purse and extracted several papers. "All of the purchase-and-sale agreements were printed on Churchill, Walmer, and Pickwick pleading paper."

Raine set the autopsy report down on the bench and took the papers from Sommers. Sure enough, every sales agreement had the law firm's name and address in the lower right corner. He flipped through to see who the specific attorneys were.

"None of these were prepared by Amanda Stone," he noted.

"I would hope not," Sommers answered. "She's a personal injury litigation attorney. She has no business drafting documents for multi-million-dollar real estate contracts. But her firm sure does."

Raine supposed that was true. "But it's not the same purchaser?"

Sommers motioned to the papers in Raine's hand. "You can't really tell from these. I need to do more digging. Each business had a different purchaser, but each purchaser was a corporation. It could be the same people behind it."

"Who bought the first place?" Raine asked. He could have searched the documents, but he knew Sommers had the information at her fingertips.

"MarQet Capital, LLC," she answered. "Market with a 'Q'."

"That's annoying," Raine said. "I thought the trend of intentionally misspelling things was over."

"It should be," Sommers agreed. "The former bookstore was bought by a company called CNM Investments."

"CNM?" Raine asked. "That sounds like a stock market abbreviation for cinnamon. Is it a food company or something?"

Sommers shrugged. "I don't know yet."

"Who bought the last place?"

"Shiboo, Incorporated," Sommers answered.

"Shiboo?" Raine repeated. "What's that mean?"

"No idea," Sommers admitted.

"Sounds foreign," Raine suggested. "Overseas investors maybe?"

But Sommers shook her head. "I doubt it. If it was really foreign, it would be spelled with a 'u' not double-'o'. Double-'o' is a uniquely English way to spell that sound, but it's a nonsense word in English."

"That's a very subtle observation," Raine admired. He bit into the cone holding the remainder of his sherbet.

"I deal in subtleties," Sommers answered, "and extravagancies. Each have their uses in my line of work."

"So, we need to find out who's behind those corporations. It's either an amazing coincidence or a plan."

"It's a plan," Sommers answered. "Owning three out of four buildings on a block means steady rental income. Owning all of them means you can sell for a small fortune to a developer ready to build the city's next office-tower."

"Stone's firm has a client who wants Duncan's gallery," Raine realized. "But they want it at a discount."

"Nothing drives a price down like a dead body," Sommers remarked. She looked at the manilla folder on the bench. "What does the autopsy report say? Any help?"

Raine handed her the report. "It's about as unhelpful as possible," he complained. "If it said with absolute certainty that it was suicide, I might actually be able to convince

Castro to allow for a second, albeit belated, opinion. If it was fifty-fifty, maybe suicide or maybe murder, then that would have been great in front of the jury."

"So, what does it say?" Sommers extracted the report, but held it gingerly at arm's length.

Wise, Raine thought. The last several pages were photographs of the autopsy.

"It says it was probably suicide," Raine answered. "Like very, very probably suicide. I can have another expert review it and testify as to any deficiencies in method or conclusion, but I won't be able to exhume the body on this."

"Well, it's something," Sommers returned the pages to the envelope and traded Raine for her purchase-and-sale agreements. "Do you have an expert in mind? Who does that kind of thing?"

"There are private pathologists," Raine answered. "Ones who work at hospitals or even hospices. Maybe a retired medical examiner looking to make a little cash on the side. But that's the other problem."

"What?" Sommers asked.

"Payment," Raine answered. "They aren't going to testify out of the goodness of their hearts. Finch is going to have to pay them and I don't think he's going to be able to."

"Why not?"

"Because he hasn't paid me," Raine answered. "He's late on his next retainer."

"Oh dear," Sommers commented.

"Exactly," Raine answered. "We need to schedule a little talk with Duncan Finch."

13

Raine didn't tell Finch why he needed to meet with him. They both knew. There weren't a lot of reasons for insisting on a meeting on a Friday afternoon. The only thing Finch didn't know was that Sommers was going to be there too. Raine certainly could have conducted a 'you owe me money' conversation on his own, and without breaking Finch's other hand. But having a third party present, especially a friend, would increase the shame of not paying. And shame was Raine's strongest weapon in extracting his fee from Finch. That, and the threat of quitting.

"We need to talk about money, Duncan," Raine got right to it. "Your retainer account dropped below five thousand. I sent you an invoice, but you never added any funds. Now it's down to less than a thousand. I can't do any more work on the case until you replenish the funds."

Finch frowned as his eyes darted between Raine and Sommers. He fidgeted with the cast on his hand. "I know, I know," Finch answered. "And I know I promised you I wouldn't be late, but some things came up, and it's just... ever since that suicide at the fundraiser, I'm having trouble booking new events. No one wants to do a showing where there was a dead body."

"Told ya," Sommers remarked to Raine.

Raine pointed at the cast. "And you have other creditors who take precedence over me."

Finch looked down at his broken hand. His frown deepened. But he didn't deny it. "Yes."

"You're going to lose the gallery if you don't win this case," Sommers said.

"And you won't win this case if we don't give it everything we can," Raine added. "That means paying not just me, but expert witnesses."

"Like a psychologist to testify about how one person can't really drive another person to suicide?" Finch asked.

"No," Raine answered, "although that's not a terrible idea. But that would mean hiring two experts, and first we have to figure out how you're going to afford one."

"Which one?" Finch asked.

"A forensic pathologist," Raine answered, "to testify that Hailey Parker's death might have been a homicide after all."

"They'll say that?" Finch's frown suddenly turned to a hopeful smile.

"Not if we don't pay them," Raine replied. "And maybe not if we do. We don't pay for the opinion we want. We pay them to get the opinion they have, and if we like it, we pay them again to testify to it at trial."

"That sounds like a lot of money." Finch's expression fell again.

"It is," Raine confirmed.

"I don't have a lot of money," Finch admitted. "I can't even pay you."

That was the last thing Raine wanted to hear. They could try to win without the experts, but he wasn't going to do the case for free. Not even for one of Sommers's friends. Amanda Stone and her law firm's secret client would be buying his building next. Sommers might even broker the transaction, since she'd be out of a job too as his investigator.

"We need to raise the money, then," Sommers put in.

"Raise it?" Raine questioned. "Like a bake sale?"

Sommers grinned. "Actually, yes, very much like a bake sale."

Raine wasn't sure he liked Sommers's smile, but he trusted it.

"I really think that gala could have been successful, if it hadn't been for..." Sommers started.

"If it hadn't been for the dead girl in the bathroom?"

"Well, yes," Sommers said. "If we could do that again, but have the proceeds go to Duncan, he could earn more than enough to pay you and the expert."

"Experts?" Finch suggested hopefully.

Raine appreciated the idea, but he wasn't convinced. "Why would Selina agree to do a fundraiser for someone else?"

"Okay, they can split it," Sommers allowed. "We just need to get that lightning back into the bottle for one night."

Raine considered for a moment. "I mean, I guess Cascadia didn't get anything from the first fundraiser. Everyone left before the bidding started."

"Exactly!" Sommers was genuinely excited.

Raine got an idea. A terrible idea, but still, an idea. "And if we intentionally exclude some of the students whose artwork was better than Hailey's, and they don't kill themselves in the bathroom over it, we'll have additional evidence that Duncan isn't at fault for Hailey Parker's decision."

Finch just blinked at Raine.

Sommers took a moment, then said, "Wow."

"Too much?" Raine asked.

"No, I'm just surprised," Sommers said. "It's brilliant."

"You're surprised I'm brilliant?" Raine raised an eyebrow at her.

"Don't get ahead of yourself." Sommers put up a hand. "We still need Selina to agree."

"And," Finch added, "we need for no one to kill themselves in my bathroom again."

Raine was about to guarantee at least that much, but he stopped himself. He didn't want to jinx it. The last thing they needed was to get sued by two sets of parents.

14

Raine and Sommers decided to go directly to the Cascadia Art School after their meeting with Finch, before everyone in Seattle began going home for the weekend. They didn't call first. That was intentional. Everything with Sommers was intentional, Raine was beginning to realize.

"If she's going to say no, we need to make her say it to our faces," Sommers explained, "and not give her time to think about it."

"Agreed," Raine replied. "Should we both go, or just me?"

"Definitely both of us," Sommers answered. "I know how to close a deal. Just be a good lawyer and stay quiet until you're needed."

"Oh?" Raine was bemused by the thought of being sidelined in his own case. "And when might that be?"

"You'll know," Sommers ended the conversation. "Now, let's go, but we need to drive separately. I have a meeting across town this afternoon and I don't want to have to drive back here."

"Fine with me," Raine replied. "I'll be a good lawyer and get there faster than you. I'll meet you at the main entrance."

"Sounds like a race." Sommers grinned. "May the best person win."

Raine smiled back. "Remember, I know how to beat a speeding ticket."

Sommers shook out her long blonde hair and smoothed her perfect outfit. "And I know how to avoid getting a ticket in the first place."

————

IN THE EVENT, neither of them got a ticket and Raine got there first, albeit by less than a minute. He was just walking away from his car when Sommers drove past him to find an even closer parking spot.

"I win!" she called out as he approached the car.

"I was here first," Raine pointed out.

"But I'm closer," Sommers argued, jumping out of her car.

Raine frowned slightly. "Sounds like we were running two different races."

"Well, I won mine." Sommers grinned. "That's what matters."

"I think what matters is what's about to happen in there." Raine pointed at the art school ahead of them. "Not what happens out here."

"They can both matter," Sommers replied. "And anyway, I'm not as confident we're going to convince Selina to help us win in there."

"We don't have to convince her to help us win," Raine said. "We have to convince her she'll win too."

Most legal cases, civil or criminal, settled far short of trial. The conventional wisdom was that you could tell a fair deal if both sides were disappointed. Raine preferred to subscribe to the theory that a fair deal meant both sides felt like they'd won, even if it was at the expense of the other. Maybe especially if it was at the expense of the other. Raine didn't necessarily have to persuade Thorne that a second gallery fundraiser was good for her, as long as he could persuade her that it was better for her than it was for someone else. He just wasn't sure who that someone else was for Thorne. Was it Finch? Was it him? Or someone else he didn't even know or had already forgotten about?

The main doors to the school were unlocked and there was no one waiting for them when they entered the facility. Devoid of students in the hallways, the school had that feeling only schools had when classes were in session and everyone was hidden away in the classrooms. A combination of quiet and expectation. Vibrance, on pause. So quiet it felt wrong to even speak aloud.

Sommers pointed at a sign that read, 'MAIN OFFICE '. Raine nodded and they made their way down the hall, silent save the clack of their shoes on the linoleum, Raine's dress shoes a dull beat, Sommers's heels a sharp staccato. The corridor turned twice, once right then left, before they came to the large wooden door of the main office. Raine almost felt as if he should knock, but Sommers apparently held no such compunctions. She pushed the door open to reveal not just Selina Thorne, their intended target, but Caleb Marquardt, whom Raine had all but forgotten.

They were alone in the antechamber just outside Thorne's actual office. The area where the school secretary sat and the coffee percolated. Where students would wait to meet with the Head of School. But there was no secretary and no students in the room. Just Thorne and Marquardt.

Raine couldn't help but notice how they were standing. A little too close, he thought. With Marquardt leaning in to stand a bit closer to Thorne, but Thorne trying to create some distance between them, although only perhaps because of their sudden observation by someone else. It was almost as if Marquardt were trying to hide something they were standing in front of, and Thorne was willing to let it be seen lest someone conclude their proximity meant something more. All Raine knew for sure was that he didn't like it very much.

"What are you doing here?"

It was a question any one of them might have asked any other of them, but it was posed simultaneously by Thorne to Raine and Sommers, and by Sommers to Marquardt.

"We're here with a business proposition," Raine answered first.

Marquardt smiled. "That's also why I'm here. How fortuitous."

Raine glanced at Thorne. She didn't confirm Marquardt's assertion, but she didn't deny it either. She just seemed relieved somehow.

"Shall we all go into my office then?" she suggested. "Perhaps our interests are aligned."

Raine looked to Sommers for her reaction. She had no hesitation.

"Sounds perfect," Sommers agreed. "Do you have any more of that chai?"

Thorne smiled broadly. She had a very nice smile. "Always."

Thorne's office was really more of a living room. There

was a desk to be sure, but it was almost hidden in the corner. The real work was done around the table at the center of the space. Raine, Sommers, and Marquardt sat down in the low, upholstered chairs while Thorne fetched the tray of chai. In a few moments, they were seated around the table, drinks in hand.

"So, Rebecca, Daniel, let's hear your idea first," Thorne invited. "I'm already bored to death of Caleb and his incessant proposals."

Marquardt surrendered a pained smile at the barb.

Raine was curious what Caleb's proposals entailed, but he didn't mind getting right to his own business. "We want to do another show."

"Another fundraiser," Sommers clarified. "At Duncan's gallery."

Thorne frowned over her chai. "The last one did not end particularly well."

"All the more reason to try again," Sommers argued.

"We think it would be beneficial to Duncan's case," Raine explained. "Duncan is willing to do it again, if you are."

Thorne sipped thoughtfully from her mug. "I'm not sure my students will be."

But Caleb seemed excited by the idea. "Oh, nonsense, Selina. Your students were cheated out of their big night. They deserve a do-over."

"It seems disrespectful," Thorne continued to resist. "Do we all just pretend Hailey didn't take her own life that night?"

"We could dedicate the evening to her," Sommers suggested.

Raine wasn't sure about that notion. "I'm not sure we can dedicate it to the person who's suing our client."

"Technically, her parents are the ones suing," Sommers pointed out.

"Still seems a bit tacky," Raine opined.

But Thorne seemed to warm to the idea. "I'm not part of whatever your lawsuit is. I'm just a simple art teacher. I agree that my students were cheated out of their big night. I also think we should do something for Hailey. It was all so terrible, and then this lawsuit. We never took the time to mourn her, let alone honor her."

"Exactly," Marquardt agreed heartily. "I can see it already. We could put a memorial at the front entrance. A large portrait of her, perhaps. Flowers, certainly. Oh!" He darted a finger into the air. "We could create a scholarship in her name! I will even make the first donation."

"Oh, Caleb." Thorne placed a hand on his arm. "That's so good of you."

Raine was trying to keep up with the evolving event, assessing how it might impact his defense of Finch. Central to that was Finch's ability to pay him.

"Let's slow down a bit," he cautioned. "I'm concerned Hailey's parents will accuse Duncan of abusing her memory for financial gain."

"Duncan?" Thorne asked. "He wouldn't benefit from a scholarship fund. I don't believe he was planning on applying to my school."

Raine frowned slightly. "Part of this proposal is to raise money for Duncan's legal defense."

Thorne raised an eyebrow. "Ah. So, your financial gain."

"My fee," Raine countered. "Not anything more than I charge for doing my job. But Duncan is having some cash-flow issues. Apparently it's hard to book new shows after someone dies in your gallery."

"What happened that night wasn't Duncan's fault," Sommers put in. "He doesn't deserve any of this, but he does deserve a vigorous defense."

Thorne set her mug down. "I'm not sure I see how this helps his defense, other than to pay you two."

Raine sighed and looked to Sommers, who nodded in return. "We were thinking that if perhaps we limited the students whose art was displayed, and none of them killed themselves, it would show that the plaintiffs' theory of the case isn't tenable."

Raine waited for a reaction. Thorne waited to provide it. Her face was expressionless as she considered what she had just been told.

Marquardt was less reserved. "That does make sense," he said. "I almost admire the cold calculation of it."

"Well, I don't." Thorne crossed her arms. "I support a memorial for Hailey. I love the idea of a scholarship in her name. And I guess I'm fine with Duncan raising money for himself. But I draw the line at intentionally hurting any of my students. If we do this, then one of my conditions is that anyone who wants their artwork displayed gets that opportunity. No exceptions."

Raine looked again to Sommers.

"Your call," she said. "You know best how to help Duncan's case."

Raine did the math in his head. Or rather, the evidence rules. If he'd been any good at math, he wouldn't have gone to law school. But he was pretty good at analyzing the admissibility of potential evidence in a trial. It would have been a long shot to get a judge to let him tell a jury that no one else killed themselves at the second fundraiser. It was an attenuated argument at best. He wouldn't be losing much if he agreed to Thorne's condition. Especially when the alternative was Finch not paying him.

"Okay," Raine agreed. "Let's do it your way. Patrons can donate to a scholarship fund in Hailey's name. We sell everything on the walls and split the profits fifty-fifty between The Finch Gallery and Cascadia Art School."

"One third, one third, one third," Thorne countered. "Duncan, my school, and the student."

"No," Raine said.

"No?" Thorne seemed taken aback.

"No," Raine repeated. "That won't be enough for Duncan. For my fee. Half for him. You can split the other half however you want. Otherwise it's not worth the time and effort."

Thorne turned to Caleb. "What do you think?"

Marquardt thought for a moment. "I think that's a fair compromise. No one gets everything they want, but perhaps everyone gets what they need. That's usually the best deal."

Raine appreciated Marquardt's appraisal. Thorne seemed to, as well.

"Fine." She extended a hand across the table. "We have a deal."

Raine gladly shook it. She really did have a pleasantly warm hand.

"But," Thorne cautioned, "I can't guarantee how many of my students will want to participate, given what occurred previously."

"Understood," Raine said, "but I expect you can be very persuasive when you want to be."

Thorne smiled warmly at Raine, then looked shyly away.

Raine found it inviting. The others perhaps less so.

"So," Sommers cleared her throat, "what was Caleb's proposal?"

"Uh," Marquardt hesitated, with a glance to Thorne.

Thorne was brought fully back to the conversation. "Nothing nearly as exciting as this," she assured. "Caleb simply needs some artwork for his new office and was trying to talk my price down."

"Oh, your own artwork?" Sommers asked. "I'd love to see more of that."

"I'm very selective about displaying my own work," Thorne demurred. "But perhaps I will offer a piece for our new endeavor."

Another part of reaching an agreement was ending the conversation before anyone changed their mind. Raine had what he'd come for—most of it anyway. It was time to end the visit.

Raine stood up. "I believe we've taken up enough of your time," he announced. "We should be going. Let you two return to whatever negotiations we interrupted."

Marquardt seemed to like that idea, but Thorne not so much. "I'm afraid I must return to work. I will escort all three of you out."

Raine was glad to see that Thorne didn't seem to be interested in Marquardt after all. He decided to take a risk. "Rebecca, could you tell Caleb about our plans regarding a sponsor for the show? I agree. I think he'd be perfect."

Sommers raised a surprised eyebrow, but she was a good partner. "Of course, Dan," she replied. "Caleb, darling, would you be willing to step outside? I want to make sure I have your undivided attention."

Marquardt's head spun as if on a swivel, from Sommers to Raine to Thorne and back to Sommers again.

"Free advertising," Sommers coaxed.

"Free advertising," Marquardt repeated, trancelike. "All right. Yes. Let's step outside. I'm eager to hear about this sponsorship opportunity."

Sommers guided Marquardt out of the office and Raine turned back to Thorne.

She tucked her red hair behind her ear and nodded admiringly. "Very impressive. I've been trying to get him to leave for over an hour."

"You just have to know what motivates people," Raine replied. "He's clearly motivated by a beautiful woman, but he's more motivated by money."

"You flatter me," Thorne said, with a shy grin. "And what motivates you?"

Raine saw no reason to be anything other than honest. "I'd like to get to know you better, and I was wondering whether you might be free for dinner tonight."

Selina took a few moments before answering. Thoughts raced unexpressed behind her bright eyes. Finally, she smiled again, and gave her answer. "Like I said, you flatter me. But I feel a little strange about it, given all of the circumstances. You represent a friend, partnered with another friend, against a lawsuit by the parents of one of my students. I'm sure I will end up being a witness, one way or another. So I think it's probably best if we keep things professional."

Raine supposed he should have expected that response. He could even respect it. "Professional," he repeated.

"Distant," Thorne clarified. "At least until this terrible litigation is over."

Raine nodded, mostly to himself. "I can appreciate that.

Thanks for being honest. And ethical. I'll look forward to seeing you again, professionally."

Thorne smiled again, but weakly. "I'll look forward to that too, Daniel."

Raine took his leave and made his way out of the school. When he reached the fading daylight, Sommers was waiting for him, alone.

"How'd it go?" she asked. "Do you have a date with Madame Thorne?"

"I do not," Raine admitted. "She felt it better to keep things professional, at least while the case is pending."

"Ah," Sommers replied.

"Probably just as well," Raine consoled himself. "I have the boys this weekend. I probably shouldn't show up at Natalie's tomorrow morning smelling like perfume and alcohol."

"If you say so." Sommers avoided commenting on Raine's personal life.

Raine supposed he appreciated that. "What about Caleb?" he changed the subject. "What did we give him?"

"A sign promoting his business, placed conspicuously in the main gallery," Sommers answered, "and an ad on the back of the program."

"What is his business, exactly?" Raine asked.

"I'm not sure actually," Sommers confessed. "Something to do with imports and exports, I think."

"Fantastic. I struck out, and Caleb's business logo will mar our event," Raine summarized.

"Lose-lose," Sommers added. She checked her phone. "It's almost time for my next appointment. I need to leave."

Raine sighed and ran a hand through his hair. "And I need a drink."

15

The Cascadia Art School was only a few blocks from Seattle's Belltown neighborhood. The area had once been known as 'The Denny Regrade' because some of the early settlers of Rain City had decided to flatten the former Denny Hill into a tabula rasa they hoped would be a boon for business north of downtown. Instead, it mostly became a transitory area between downtown and the decidedly not-flattened Queen Anne Hill, one of Seattle's most prestigious neighborhoods, past and present. It wasn't until the area filled with dive bars and those dive bars filled with what would eventually be termed 'Grunge' bands that the neighborhood finally reached its envisioned potential. All of that meant Raine could leave his car where he had parked and walk to where he was going to drink, wherever that ended up being.

It was Friday night, but it was early. Later on, no doubt most of the bars would have lines out the door, throngs of twenty-somethings crowding into club after club to see the latest local band lucky enough to book a gig at one of the neighborhood's myriad venues. Until then, Raine had his pick of places. He reached First Avenue and looked up and down the street, hoping to discern some indication of which establishment might offer someone of his age a good drink and adequate food. Two good drinks. Maybe more. He would see how the night developed.

As he reflected on not being familiar with the nightlife in Belltown, he realized he wasn't really familiar with any of the nightlife anywhere in Seattle. Such was the lot of a married lawyer with two kids. But then again, he was single now. And Thorne had turned him down. He decided to pass on the place for someone his age and sought out a club with people decidedly more interesting than himself. He tried not to be depressed at how easy that task would be.

After a trip up and down the main three blocks of bars, he settled on a place on the corner of First Avenue and Battery Street. The Quarry. There was already music spilling out of the doors and the people milling about outside seemed to be far closer in age to Thorne's students than the headmistress herself. He expected the drinks to be strong and the food minimal. Perfect.

There was even a bouncer at the front door, but given the hour, there was no need to keep anyone out until others had left. He was a young guy, also twenty-something, with biceps the size of Raine's legs. Larger, probably. Raine expected a snide grin from the young man, but he simply opened the door for him and offered a polite, "Evening, sir."

Inside, it was very dark and very loud. There was a band on the small stage jammed into one corner of the single large room. Raine admired their eagerness, but it was obvious why they were the first warm-up act. Flashing colored lights around the perimeter of the ceiling offered enough light for Raine to navigate his way to the bar. There was nowhere else to sit anyway. There was an arc of tall, metal tables, but none of them had chairs. It was going to be standing room only eventually, he deduced. So, he pulled up a stool at the end of the bar and waited for the bartender to make his way over to him. Neither of them seemed to be in any rush.

Raine people-watched while he waited. The people inside the bar seemed to be about fifty-fifty patrons and staff, both groups getting ready in their own way for whatever would be coming later. Raine was looking forward to finding that out as well.

"Hey there," the bartender greeted him when he finally made his way over to the end of the bar. He was a little on the short side, with a shaved head and a neatly trimmed red beard. He wore a burgundy vest over a crisp white shirt, the sleeves rolled up to reveal tattoo sleeves on both arms, along with several more tattoos on his hands and knuckles. He set two cardboard coasters in front of Raine and started pouring him a glass of water. "What are you drinking tonight?"

Raine considered ordering his usual: an Old Fashioned. Or maybe he would go crazy and get a Manhattan. But he wasn't there to experience the same thing he always did. That would come tomorrow morning at Nat's. He was out to experience something new. "What do you recommend?" he asked. "I'd like to try something a little different."

The bartender set down Raine's glass of water and rubbed his chin. "Something a little different, eh? Are you a whiskey man? Or maybe gin?"

"Whiskey," Raine fairly admitted. He didn't want to be easy to read. Not that night.

"You prefer something sweet or something dry?" the bartender continued his inquiry.

"Surprise me," Raine answered. "It doesn't even have to be whiskey. Just something good. And strong."

The bartender nodded. "All right, my friend. I'll mix you up something special. And strong."

Raine thanked the bartender and turned again to watch the door. There were more women than men, and most of them were already a little unsteady on their feet. One of the women started laughing at something another woman said and lost her balance, almost falling off her four-inch heels. Before Raine could rush over to help, she righted herself and slapped the woman who had made her laugh, as if it were her fault she had almost fallen. They looked like they were having fun.

"Here you are!" The bartender returned with the concoction he had mixed for Raine. He set it on the empty coaster and pushed it toward him. "Tell me what you think."

"What is it?" Raine asked even as he picked up the glass and raised it to his mouth.

"Taste it first," the bartender directed. "I don't want to spoil the surprise."

Raine could appreciate a good surprise. More importantly, he could appreciate a good drink. He took a long sip. That was a good drink. "This is fantastic! What's in it?"

"I decided not to use whiskey as the base spirit," the bartender explained. "You look like you always drink something whiskey-based. So, it's rum-based, with some lime juice, sugar, ginger liqueur, and a few other things to balance it out."

Raine took a second, deeper drink. "This is really good. It's sweet."

The bartender smiled and nodded. "Something new for you. I hope you find whatever else you're hoping to find tonight. Let me know when you're ready for another drink. I've got an idea for something a little drier."

Raine was almost finished with the drink already. He wasn't sure they needed to move from sweet to dry quite so fast, but he definitely trusted the bartender. He took a moment to breathe and looked around the club again.

It was starting to fill up, a bit quicker than Raine had expected based on how dead it was when he arrived not too much earlier. All of the chairless tables had been claimed and the band that had been playing when he arrived was finishing up their set. A quiet rolled through the space as they started to pack up their instruments and the next band hovered near the stage, eager to keep things going. Raine returned his attention to the bar top in front of him. Not that there was anything even remotely interesting about it, but he knew he'd be the creepy old guy at the bar if he stared out at the youngins for too long.

The bartender's second drink was tequila-based and sweeter than Raine had feared. It was also at least as strong as the rum drink and Raine was starting to feel the effect of two bespoke cocktails and no food. He raised a hand to try to get the attention of the bartender, but lowered it again as a young woman stepped up to the bar near him. The second band started to play, so Raine was going to have to yell.

"Hello!" he called out to the young woman. She was the same age as everyone else there but him, with black hair and dramatic makeup. She was also the art student he'd met briefly along with Hailey Parker the night of her death. "Veronica, right? Veronica Kwon."

Veronica Kwon narrowed her eyes at the old man at the bar. "Do I know you?"

Raine shrugged. "We met. Once. I'm Dan. You're a student at the Cascadia Art School, right? I was at that fundraiser gala thing." He supposed he should go ahead and say it, lest he seem like a psychopath for not caring about the most important thing that happened that night. "The one where Hailey died."

"Oh," Kwon replied. "Okay. Yeah, I don't really remember you. Sorry."

Raine supposed he shouldn't be surprised. Or offended. "That's alright. I just recognized you so I thought I would say hello." He glanced over at the people milling about and dancing in the rest of the club. "I was just talking with your school director about maybe doing another fundraiser."

The bartender stepped up at that moment to take Kwon's order. There would be no special cocktail for her. She just wanted three beers, one whiskey and coke, and a vodka and cranberry juice. Raine appreciated what the bartender had done for him even more after hearing Kwon's order. The bartender departed to prepare the drinks, so they were forced to keep making conversation.

"Is there really going to be another show?" Kwon asked.

Raine shrugged. "If enough students want to do it. Selina —Ms. Thorne—said that would be the tricky part. She thought you students would be conflicted between wanting to have a proper gallery showing after all, but not wanting to dishonor Hailey's memory."

Kwon nodded. "Yeah, that kinda makes sense."

"So, I guess they're going to start a scholarship fund in her name," Raine continued to recount his earlier conversation. "I'm not exactly sure about that. That's not really my department."

"Oh yeah?" Kwon laughed. She seemed to be deciding that he wasn't a creep after all. "What's your department?"

Raine had been drinking, and the drinks had been strong, but he wasn't drunk enough to tell Kwon he was the lawyer fighting against her dead friend's parents. "Not business," he answered. "I'm far more interested in the art."

"Oh really?" Kwon perked up. "Did you see anything you liked at the show? I mean, you know, before what happened happened."

Raine was beginning to weave a tangled web. He needed to divert the conversation away from himself because the truth was he hadn't paid much attention to the art that night. But he did remember hers.

"I recall a landscape," he said. "Well, actually it was a waterscape. Is that a word? It was of ocean waves striking a beach at night. It was realistic but also not completely realistic, but in a good way. I liked that one very much."

"What did you like about it?" Kwon asked.

Raine thought for a moment. Just because he wasn't divulging his connection to the lawsuit arising out of that evening didn't mean he had to lie about everything.

"I liked how it made me feel," he answered. "Alone, but not exactly lonely." He held up his drink. "Like there was a rinse of loneliness in the glass, but then it was filled with self-reliance. And a recognition of the permanence of things larger than ourselves."

Kwon's eyebrows rose up. "You got all that from my painting?"

"It was your painting?" Raine feigned surprise. "Wow. You're very good."

"Well, thank you," Kwon said.

The bartender brought her drinks then, arranged tidily on a cork-lined tray.

Kwon looked at the drinks, then Raine, then out onto the floor where her friends ostensibly were, then back at Raine again. "Would you like to come over and meet my friends? We're all students at Cascadia. Maybe you could see if they'd be interested in doing another gallery show."

Raine thought that was a great idea. He picked up his drink and followed Kwon into the crowd. He was impressed by Kwon's ability to navigate the undulating mass of attendees without spilling even a drop of the drinks she was carrying. For his part, Raine was barely able to keep his drink in his glass with all of the people bumping into him. Fortunately, they soon reached the table where Kwon's friends were waiting for her. They seemed glad to see her return, even gladder to see their drinks, and suspicious of the middle-aged man who had followed her.

"You okay, V?" one of the young men asked.

Very chivalrous of him, but Raine had no doubt he could take the youngster in a fight. He had several inches and a couple dozen pounds on him, plus the strength that comes from years of disillusionment and disappointment.

"I'm fine, Evan," Kwon waved away his concern. "This is Dan. He's friends with Selina."

A chorus of "Oh"s circled the table. Instant credibility. Raine thought it was nice that Thorne's students liked her so much.

"Dan says they might do another gallery showing," Kwon continued. "If enough of us are willing to do it."

Several of the assembled friends cringed, muttering reservations at the idea.

"I don't know," one of the women summarized their thoughts. She had short white hair with purple tips and black lipstick. "Doesn't that sort of disrespect Hailey's memory or whatever?"

"They're gonna do a scholarship fund," Kwon yelled over the music. "Like, a whole memorial thing and everything."

Raine raised a cautionary hand. "The details are still being worked out, but yeah, Ms. Thorne wants to make sure it's handled respectfully. She also wants you all to get the opportunity to show your work again."

Another of the young men in the group frowned. "Isn't her family, like... like pissed at the gallery, though? I heard they were suing or something."

Kwon looked to Raine. "Is that true?"

He took a beat. There were two options, and neither of them was good. Telling them the truth, and his role in the lawsuit, would let every student at the school know that the fundraiser was being organized by the man Hailey's parents blamed for her death, or worse yet, by that man's lawyer. The request really needed to come from Thorne. On the other hand, lying about it was likely to come back to bite him at some point.

He could just imagine Amanda Stone examining Veronica Kwon at the trial. *Isn't it true that the attorney for the defendant, Mr. Raine, lied to you about profiting off the memory of my clients' dead daughter?*

Yes, that's true. He also was like twice the age of everyone else in the club that night.

Raine needed a third option. He set his drink down on the table and shouted. "Where are the bathrooms?"

The band had finished their latest song immediately

before Raine belted out his question, so everyone in the club knew he needed to pee.

Kwon laughed at the happenstance. She pointed to a hallway past the bar. "They're down that hallway."

Raine's "Thank you" was smothered by the beginning of the next song, so he just shrugged and made his way across the crowded floor. It wasn't just a ruse to avoid answering questions about who was defending whom against which lawsuit filed by whose parents. He really did need to use the bathroom. The timing was simply fortuitous. He expected that by the time he got back to the table, Kwon's group would have moved on to a new topic of conversation. He also expected he'd pay his tab and head home. He needed to be at Natalie's at 9:00 tomorrow morning to pick up his boys.

There was a line for the urinals, but it moved quickly enough. Raine relieved himself, washed his hands, avoided his own gaze in the mirror, and headed back onto the floor. When he got back to the table, the woman with the white and purple hair and a few others were still there, but Kwon was nowhere in sight.

"Did Veronica leave?" Raine asked over the music.

The white-and-purple-haired woman shrugged. "I'm not sure."

The others didn't add anything.

It was time to leave. He picked his drink up off the table and drained the better portion of what was left. "Nice meeting you all," he offered in departure.

The others offered a mixed bag of half-smiles and noncommittal shrugs. It was definitely time to go home.

He made his way back to the bar and let the bartender know he was ready to close out his tab. He finished his drink, gave the bartender a credit card.

A minute or two later he had his card back and headed toward the exit. The music was getting louder and the lights more blinding. He squinted against the strobe as he pushed past the people between him and fresh air. The front door seemed impossibly far away. He was sweating from the heat of the crowd pressed against him. He began pulling past people like a swimmer pulling at the water. He was aware of people complaining at being touched, but their words were distant. He just needed to get outside.

He broke the plane of the door and stumbled out into the night. The air was cool, but it didn't stop the heat running up his back and over the top of his head. The lights from the street spun and melted together. He looked up to find the moon. It wasn't there. Or maybe it was. The entire world spun around him and he lost his balance.

This is gonna hurt, was his last thought before his head hit the sidewalk.

16

When Raine woke up, he couldn't see. Or rather, he didn't dare open his eyes. His head felt like it was split down the middle, held together by metal hooks. Even the minimal act of moving his eyelids threatened to increase the pain beyond what was already an unbearable level. On top of that, there was a horrific level of brightness burning just past his eyelids. He felt certain he couldn't bear the pain that would come if any light waves struck his retina. He wasn't aware of anything beyond the immediacy of the crushing pain in his head. He raised an arm to drape over his eyes and let out a low groan.

"Are you awake?" a woman's voice asked. "How are you feeling?"

Raine didn't recognize the voice. It wasn't Nat. It wasn't Rebecca. It wasn't even Selina. He let out a long sigh. He was going to have to open his eyes after all.

When he did, he had no idea where he was. Not specifically, anyway. Generally, he was in an apartment. The windows were covered with disappointingly inadequate shades of gauzy fabric. The walls were covered in a random mosaic of drawings and paintings, none of which he particularly liked, although there were a few with random intersecting geometric lines that seemed to soothe his headache somehow. A tilt of that aching head confirmed he was on a bed, or rather a mattress on the floor. He realized he wasn't wearing a shirt. He reached under the single sheet draped over his form and was at least able to confirm he was wearing pants.

"Dan?" the voice asked. "Are you okay?"

Raine forced his face toward the voice and squinted through throbbing eyes. "Veronica?"

It was indeed Veronica Kwon. He was in Veronica Kwon's apartment. He was in Veronica Kwon's bed. He was half naked. And he had no memory of how he got there or what they did. Did they do something?

"Did we...?" he croaked.

Kwon laughed. "Uh no, Dan. No. Definitely not. You're not exactly my type. You're more like my mom's type."

That hurt even more than the blinding light slicing in from the windows. Sunlight. Daylight. Day time. *Oh crap*.

"What time is it?" He tried to sit up. That was a bad idea. He quickly lay down again.

"Uh, eight-fifteen," Kwon answered. "Well, almost eight-thirty."

Raine's heart slowed a bit. He hadn't missed picking up the boys. Not yet anyway. He wasn't ready to sit up yet, let alone drive. "What happened? How did I get here?" Then, after a moment, "And where is my shirt?"

"Yeah, so all of those are kind of related," Kwon

answered. She sat down on the bed, sending it reeling in Raine's estimation. He braced against the motion and waited for the explanation. "So, um, I think one of my friends thought it would be funny to spike your drink. Either that or someone did it when they weren't looking. But either way, someone put something in your drink while you were in the bathroom. You never leave your drink alone, man. You'd know that if you were a woman."

Raine thought that was a terrible thing to have to know. He also thought it was a terrible thing for someone to have done to him. He suspected the little guy who had puffed his chest out when Raine first walked up to their table.

"Why the hell...?" he started to ask, but then he realized he didn't care. Not right then anyway. "How did I end up here?"

He was starting to feel a little better. His head was still splitting, but there seemed to be fewer meat hooks. He risked propping himself up onto an elbow. Baby steps.

"I went to the bathroom at the same time you did," Kwon explained. "When I got back, you were gone. Then someone said some old guy had fallen down outside. So I went to see if you were okay."

Raine decided to ignore yet another reference to his age. "I remember falling. Did I hit my head? Did I pass out?"

"You hit your head, but you didn't pass out," Kwon explained. "You started talking about somebody named Nat. You kept saying, 'I'm sorry, Nat. I'm sorry.' You thought I was her, whoever she is. It was actually super awkward."

"Great." It was actually worse than he'd feared. "You didn't try to track down Nat, did you? She doesn't know about this, right?"

"I have no idea who Nat is or what she knows," Kwon said. "All I know is you were totally out of it and my apartment was only two blocks away. I wasn't going to just leave you there. You could have walked in front of a car or something."

Raine nodded, and finally pushed himself into a sitting position. "Thank you." He took a moment to look more fully at his surroundings. "I like all the paintings on the wall. Very Bohemian."

"I'm not even sure what that's supposed to mean, but thanks," Kwon replied. "Most of them are mine, but a few are Hailey's. We used to paint together sometimes."

"That's nice," Raine said. Then he noticed that having sat up, the sheets had slid fully off his upper body, exposing his naked chest. "Do you know where my shirt is?"

"I'm not sure, man." Kwon raised her hands like she was being robbed and stood up off the bed again. "You must have gotten too hot during the night and taken it off yourself or something."

That seemed likely. He was covered in dried sweat. He just realized how bad his mouth tasted. His senses were returning. "I need to get out of here. I need my shirt."

"Honestly, I agree with both of those things," Kwon replied. "I'm not looking forward to explaining this to my friends. I'm sure they're already talking about me taking you back to my apartment for the night."

"But you said we didn't do anything," Raine said.

"We didn't," Kwon confirmed. "But that doesn't mean they won't talk. I mean, they won't slut-shame me or anything. They'll just want details."

"Tell them I left first thing in the morning without even saying goodbye," Raine suggested.

"I'll tell them I slept in my chair while you snored all night in my bed," she said, "with your shirt off and mumbling the name 'Nat' in your sleep."

Raine closed his eyes. It was past time he was on his way. He fortified himself against the coming effort, then pushed himself to his feet. "Thank you for not letting me die on the street. I owe you one."

"Good," Kwon accepted the proffer. "Make sure that second gallery show happens."

Raine raised his aching eyes and finally looked his savior in the face. "Oh yeah?"

"Yeah," Kwon confirmed. "I want my stuff up again. And this time, nothing is going to ruin it."

———

RAINE MANAGED to find his shirt and stumble his way out of Kwon's apartment. It was only a few blocks to his car, which was still parked where he'd left it, although with a parking ticket under the windshield wiper.

The cost of doing business, he told himself as he extracted the citation from under the wiper and climbed into his car. It was 8:49 and Nat's place—his old place—was a twenty-minute drive away. He would be late, but not significantly so. The boys probably wouldn't even be ready. Nat couldn't get mad at him for being ten minutes late, he told himself.

And he was right. She was mad because he was ten minutes late *and* he showed up looking like he'd been out all night. Which was true.

"What the hell!" was the first thing she said after getting a good look at him standing on the front porch. "I expect you to be late, but I don't expect you to come straight from a whore house."

"Whoa." Raine put his hands up. "That's a little strong, don't you think?"

"Have you seen yourself?" Nat asked him. "Have you smelled yourself?"

Raine took a quick sniff of himself. "What do I smell like?" He was either accustomed to it, or his brain still wasn't working quite right.

"You smell like alcohol and cigarettes," Nat answered. She frowned deeply then leaned in to whisper. "And another woman, Dan. You smell like another woman."

"Ah." Raine raised a finger. "I can explain."

Nat barked out a laugh. "I'm sure you can, but I'm not really interested in the details. I'll just say congratulations and ask you to rinse off in the shower before you pick up our kids smelling like whatever desperate bimbo you matched with on whatever fucking dating app you have on your phone."

"It wasn't like that, I swear," Raine insisted. "She's a student at this art school and she was just trying to help me."

"An art school student?" Nat laughed again, darkly, toward the sky. "Wow. I gave you too much credit, I guess. I figured you'd start dating all the other divorcées our age. But I've got to hand it to you, Dan. If you're going to go off the rails, go all the way, right into the kiddie pool. Did you have to buy her drinks for her, or did she have a fake I.D.?"

"You're not listening," Raine tried again.

"See how it feels?" Nat crossed her arms. "Maybe it's my turn to never listen. God knows you had enough years of being the one who never listened."

Raine took a moment. His shirt was untucked and

buttoned up wrong. He smelled like alcohol and cigarettes and Veronica Kwon. But he didn't have to explain any of that to his ex-wife, because she was his *ex*-wife. He just wasn't used to that dynamic yet. "Are the boys ready?"

"So, that's it?" Nat demanded. "We're done talking about it because you say we're done?"

"We're done talking about it because we're divorced," Raine answered. "We have kids in common, we co-parent, but that's it. I'm not obligated to explain anything else to you, especially if when I do, you don't believe me anyway. So, please, just go tell Jason and Jordan that I'm here and I will meet them in the car."

Nat didn't have a reply ready. Or more likely, she did, but she bit her tongue. "Okay. That's fine. I'll tell them you're here."

"Thanks, Nat." Raine tried to soften his tone, but it didn't matter. Nat had already disappeared into the house.

A few minutes later his two boys emerged through the front door. Raine expected Nat to bring up the rear, but there was no sign of her. He sighed to himself, then switched gears from former husband to current father.

"Hey, guys! You ready for a big weekend?"

Jordan, his thirteen-year-old, wrinkled his nose at him. "You smell weird."

"It's weed," Jason told his little brother.

"It's not—" Raine began to protest, but then he realized it might well be the smell of cannabis, either from the club or Kwon's apartment. "It's probably not weed." Then, "Wait. How do you know what weed smells like?"

Jason just rolled his eyes at his father and dropped himself into Raine's car.

Jordan stopped before getting into the car and looked at

his dad with wide eyes. "Don't let Mom find out. She won't like it."

Raine nodded. "I think you're right, son."

17

W hile Thorne and Finch, and apparently Marquardt, worked on organizing a second show at The Finch Gallery, Raine had a case to defend, and it was progressing apace. Trial was scheduled to begin in just over a month. That meant it was time for the mandatory status conference, where the lawyers were required to report to the judge regarding the status of the case and whether there were any outstanding issues that might require judicial intervention. What the judge really wanted to know was whether the case was going to settle short of trial. Based on the complete lack of negotiations since Raine had tried to dig up the dead girl, settlement seemed unlikely. That impression was reinforced when Stone entered Judge Castro's courtroom. No clients this time, but she did have three junior associates in tow. They were literally carrying her briefcase. And her files. And her coffee. Ah, life at a big firm.

"Ms. Stone," Raine greeted her as she made her way to the plaintiffs' counsel table. He had already staked out the defense table, although he had to carry his briefcase all by himself.

Stone glanced past Raine and grunted. "No Finch today?"

"Afraid not," Raine answered. "You know how clients are. If he were here, everything would take twice as long because I'd have to explain everything three times. This is better."

"I need to depose him, by the way." Stone was in no mood for small talk, it seemed. "Before the trial."

"Obviously before the trial," Raine replied. "It won't do much good afterward. Do you have any dates in mind? Since I own my practice, I have some flexibility in my schedule."

"I'll send you a notice with the date and time," Stone said. "It will be at my office. I'll have the court reporter. You bring your client."

"Well, like I said, I have some flexibility," Raine repeated, "but not complete flexibility. I don't think you can just pick a time and expect everyone to drop everything to accommodate your schedule."

Stone smiled at him. "That is exactly what I expect, Mr. Raine. And I will get it, too."

Raine nodded at her, more out of surprise than agreement. "I guess we'll see. Send me a notice. I'll tell you whether we can appear. If not, you can pick a different date."

"If not," Stone pointed at him, "then I will seek sanctions from the court for failing to comply with your discovery obligations."

Raine took a moment to slow his breathing. He hated criminal cases because of the clients, but he also kind of hated civil cases, because of the lawyers. "I feel like this hearing is going to go really well," he quipped.

They didn't have to wait long to find out. Judge Castro

was punctual, as was her reputation, and the bailiff was calling everyone to "All rise!" by 9:01 a.m.

"Are the parties ready for the status conference on the matter of *Parker v Finch*?" the judge asked once she was settled in atop the bench.

"The plaintiffs are ready, Your Honor," Stone answered first. "Amanda Stone on behalf of the plaintiffs, Mark and Susan Parker."

Castro thanked Stone and invited Raine to answer her question with a small nod to him.

"The defendant is ready as well, Your Honor," Raine answered. "I will be appearing for Mr. Finch this morning."

"And it appears the Parkers are leaving the matter to their attorney as well," Castro noted. "That should make things go quickly."

"Before we get too far into the hearing, Your Honor," Stone interjected, "there is a matter which I would like to bring to the Court's attention."

Judge Castro raised a curious eyebrow. "Of course, Ms. Stone. What is it?"

"Mr. Raine just informed me," Stone told the judge, "that he intends to prevent me from deposing his client prior to trial."

"What?" Raine blurted out. "That's not what I said."

"What did you say, Mr. Raine?" Castro inquired. She seemed concerned.

"I asked her to work with me to find a mutually agreeable date and time for the deposition," Raine answered. "Her reply was that she would set the date and time unilaterally, to which I replied—"

"To which he replied he would not attend," Stone interrupted.

"If I had a conflict," Raine expounded. "Hence my request to choose a date that worked for both of us."

"The court rules allow me to determine the time and place, Your Honor," Stone argued.

"And what about when I depose your clients?" Raine pointed out.

"We will be objecting to any deposition of Mr. and Mrs. Parker," Stone informed him, and the judge, for the first time. "Subjecting them to the stress of a confrontational deposition by the lawyer of the man responsible for the death of their child would be an abusive use of the discovery process."

Castro leaned forward and rested her chin on her fist. "So much for things going quickly." She sat up again. "Let me try to take control of this hearing again. Let's start with the most important part: the trial. Is there any reasonable probability of this case settling prior to trial?"

Raine was always open to negotiations, but he didn't get a chance to say so.

"I informed Mr. Raine of my clients' position regarding settlement negotiations prior to his motion to defile the remains of my clients' daughter," Stone said. "Mr. Raine went forward with the motion anyway—only to lose, I might add. Therefore, negotiations have concluded. The case will not settle prior to trial unless the defendant agrees to pay the amount demanded in the complaint."

"Okay, so, it's going to be a trial," Judge Castro said. "And will the parties both be ready on the currently scheduled trial date?" She glanced at a slip of paper on her desk. "It is scheduled for four weeks from Monday."

"The plaintiffs will be ready, Your Honor," Stone assured the judge. "If Mr. Raine refuses to allow us to depose his client, we will move to exclude any testimony at trial from Mr. Finch."

Castro raised that eyebrow again, this time at Raine.

He shrugged. "I'm sure it will work out, Your Honor."

Judge Castro appeared less sure.

"Although we might need a motion hearing prior to trial regarding my ability to depose the Parkers," Raine continued.

"No motion is necessary, Your Honor," Stone asserted. "We are correct in our position."

Another glance from Castro to Raine, another shrug in return.

"Okay, here's what I am going to do," the judge announced. "I am going to confirm this case for trial. I can tell from here that this case is unlikely to settle short of trial. I also think it's in everyone's best interest for the trial to take place sooner rather than later."

She looked down at the attorneys. "And here is what I am not going to do. I am not going to spend time at today's hearing speculating as to what disputes may or may not arise prior to that now-confirmed trial date. The court rules establish the method for filing motions, scheduling hearings, and giving notice. If a genuine issue arises, I feel confident you each know how to do your job."

"Very much so, Your Honor," Stone responded.

"Thank you, Your Honor," Raine added.

"Then I believe that concludes our status conference," Judge Castro declared. "I will look forward to seeing you in four weeks."

The bailiff repeated his exhortation of "All rise!" and the judge retired to her chambers.

Raine stepped over to the plaintiffs' table. "You can't

really think you get to depose my client but I don't get to depose yours. I mean, I thought you were supposed to be a smarter attorney than that."

Stone smiled, like a predator before a meal. "I am smarter than that, Mr. Raine. I'm smart enough to know that I'm getting paid on contingency. I will get the same no matter how many silly motion hearings I have to do. You, on the other hand, are paid by the hour, and your client already can't pay you. You can fight me about the date of your client's deposition or whether you get to depose my clients, but every hour you spend fighting that is another hour Finch can't pay for. And I'm going to do the same thing if you try to get Hailey's medical records. Eventually, you're going to have to either get out of the case, or scale back your defense. Either one of those is fine with me."

"Wow." Raine was actually impressed. He thought she was just being petty, but she was being strategic and cold-blooded. He needed to remember that. "How do you know Mr. Finch is having trouble paying his legal fees?"

Another grin from Stone. "I never reveal my sources. People who do that end up losing all of their sources. I'll look forward to seeing you at your client's deposition."

Stone gave a 'that's a wrap' hand signal to her minions, and they fell in line behind her as she exited the courtroom.

Raine assessed what had just happened. The issue of depositions was annoying, but he was pretty sure it was designed to be. Annoying was also distracting. The important thing was that the trial date had been confirmed. They had one month.

They really needed to get that fundraiser scheduled.

18

Raine was a lawyer, not an event planner. Luckily, between Thorne, Finch, and Sommers, they had an expert in art, an expert in displaying art, and an expert at making money off rich people.

The gala came together without a hitch—at least any hitches Raine needed to know about—and they were able to schedule it well before the trial date. That was important for several reasons, not the least of which was getting Raine's fee squared away. If Finch thought Raine had been expensive so far, wait until the trial started and he got billed by the hour for eight- to ten-hour days, every day, for several weeks. They also managed to get it scheduled before the date Amanda Stone decreed for her deposition of Finch. The last thing Raine needed was for Finch to mention the gala in his deposition and then have to deal with whatever ridiculous motion Stone filed as a result.

Raine arrived two hours early to help with the set-up. The biggest issues were where to put the display for the Hailey Parker Memorial Scholarship Fund, and where to put the sign that read 'Sponsored by Caleb Marquardt Fine Arts and Acquisitions.' The former needed to be someplace prominent enough to seem important but not so prominent as to kill the mood. The latter needed to be put somewhere no one but Marquardt would see it, but he would still be happy.

There were a lot of personalities and feelings to accommodate. Raine was actually pretty good at that. As a lawyer, he needed to care enough about his clients' cases to do a good job, but not care so much that it actually impacted him personally. He was reminded of the quote: *Sincerity is everything. If you can fake that, you've got it made.*

He placed Hailey Parker's memorial display in its own alcove in a hallway near some of the most interesting works on display that night. And he placed Marquardt's sign by the coat check. Marquardt was happy that everyone would see it as soon as they arrived; Raine knew none of them would remember it after dropping off their coats and entering the show. Win-win.

"Nice work," Sommers admired when he returned to report his accomplishments.

She was in the kitchen with Thorne and Finch. Finch was worrying at the caterers they had hired to walk around with flutes of cheap champagne and small *hors d'oeuvres* wholly inadequate to prevent the alcohol from greasing the wheels for purchases and donations. Classic fundraising technique. Sommers and Thorne seemed to be supervising Finch, from a distance, as he badgered the staff.

"Thanks," Raine replied. "I think we're ready. I hope tonight is as lucrative as the original gala might have been."

"Of course you do," Sommers laughed. "You want to get paid."

"You do realize," Raine pointed at her, "that if I don't get paid for my lawyer stuff, you don't get paid for you investigator stuff. Duncan is behind on all of his payments, for all of the things we've done on the case."

Sommers nodded. "Good point," she conceded. "I do expect to get paid."

"Speaking of the things we've done on the case," Raine continued, "were you able to get any information about who owns those companies that bought up—"

"Tut, tut, tut," Sommers interrupted him with a wag of her finger and a sidelong glance at both Thorne and Finch. "We should talk about that later. Investigator to lawyer. Tonight is about The Finch Gallery and the Cascadia Art School."

Raine took that as a sign of progress. If Sommers hadn't found any information, she simply would have said as much.

He checked the time. "Five minutes to opening," he announced. "I'm actually kind of excited about this. Let's do art!"

"Do art?" Sommers questioned.

"I kind of like it, actually," Thorne spoke up. "It's eager. And eagerness can make for a lot in life, I have found."

Raine watched Thorne's face as she spoke. Every time he thought he had forgotten about her, she appeared, looking more lovely than the last time he had seen her and complimenting him on his eagerness. Another reason to get the trial done as soon as possible.

Finch scurried over. "Is it almost time? It's almost time, isn't it? Is it time?"

"It's time," Raine confirmed. "Are you ready to open the doors of your gallery once again?"

Finch sighed. He didn't seem ready for much of

anything. "I really need tonight to be a success. Everything depends on it."

Raine was reminded of Finch's hand and the men who had broken it. He glanced at Finch's hand. He had graduated from a cast to a brace. But it was still a reminder of the precarious position Finch found himself in. He was in real danger of having to sell his gallery, and likely under market value. Probably to the Shiboo Cinnamon Market, in a deal brokered by Amanda Stone. Raine really needed to find out what Sommers had learned. But first there was a gala to kick off.

The four of them made their way from the kitchen toward the main entrance of the gallery. Raine realized Marquardt wasn't with him and he was surprised by that. Not unpleasantly so, but still, he was surprised Marquardt would be late to an event with his name on it, even if that name were relegated to the coat check.

The main hall of the gallery was filled with art students, standing eagerly next to their works of art. Although everyone was putting on a brave face and hoping for the best, it was noticeably less crowded than at the first gala. The same held true for the guests who were let in with much fanfare by Finch at exactly 7:00 p.m. There were patrons to be sure, but notably fewer than on the previous occasion. Raine could have told himself that perhaps the bulk of attendees would be fashionably late, but that would have been a lie. And if there was one person he tried not to lie to, it was himself.

Finch greeted everyone with an expansive smile and vigorous handshakes. "Welcome! Welcome! Thank you for coming!"

Raine looked over to Sommers. "Is now a good time to

talk? Everyone else will be busy with whatever they do at a thing like this."

"Sure, but let's find someplace private."

That was going to be difficult. The entire point of the gala was to get lots of people together, all throughout the gallery. They had to settle for the small kitchen again. The only other people there were the catering staff, and although some of them might be able to hear what they were saying, they were all coming and going, dropping off empty trays to return to the floor with full ones. It was unlikely that any one of them would hear their entire conversation. It was even less likely that they would be interested enough to remember anything about it.

"What did you find out?" Raine asked once they were settled into a corner as far away from anyone else as possible.

"Not as much as I'd like, I'm afraid," Sommers reported. "All three of them are privately held corporations. That significantly reduces the amount of public information they are required to provide. They don't even have to divulge who owns them."

Raine nodded. He was disappointed perhaps, but not surprised. "Did you find any connection between the three companies?"

"No. All three are based in Seattle, and they all use P.O. Boxes instead of street addresses, but the P.O. Boxes were all different, and half the corporations in the state use a Seattle mailing address."

"What about the agent for service of process?" Raine asked.

That was the person every corporation had to list who would accept service of legal documents on behalf of the company. One might think that would give some insight into who was running the company, but free enterprise had created a sub-industry of people who agreed to be service of process agents for random companies in exchange for a fee. There was nothing to do except be available in case someone wanted to sue the company, which was rare. It was easy money, and as a result there were a lot of those little businesses.

"Each of them uses a different service agency too," Sommers reported.

"Tax records?" Raine ventured.

"Those are confidential." Sommers shook her head. "I thought you would have known that."

"I do," Raine answered, "but I'm still learning the outer limits of your abilities to gather information."

"Well, it's not at tax records," Sommers assured him. "I also tracked down the agents who brokered the deals. Each one of them said they never met the buyer directly. Everything was handled through their attorneys."

"Churchill, Walmer, and Pickwick," Raine grumbled.

"Exactly," Sommers confirmed. "And they probably already have the purchase and sale agreement drafted for this place. They just need Duncan to fail."

"Or for me to," Raine noted. "If I lose this case, Duncan loses this gallery. It's as simple as that."

"At least now we know why the lawsuit was even brought," Sommers opined. "They have a client who wants to complete the purchase of this block. No matter who it is, they get paid once the deal goes through. Churchill, Walmer, and Pickwick wants to speed up the demise of The Finch Gallery."

Raine looked around at the less than stellar attendance. "They might not have to wait too much longer."

Sommers frowned at the thin crowd as well. "You know there's no way they don't know about tonight, right?"

"Amanda Stone and Churchill, Walmer, and Pickwick?" Raine confirmed that's whom she meant. "They knew I was hired almost before I did. Of course they know. In fact, I'm counting on it. If they try to make an issue about us doing this, that means telling the jury that Duncan helped fund a scholarship in Hailey's honor. It also means learning that there was a second show where no one died. Stone is smart enough to know she can't use this in court without bestowing some significant benefit on us."

"Sounds like you might be a few steps ahead of the illustrious Amanda Stone," Sommers remarked with a smile.

Raine didn't return the smile. "Or she's so far ahead of me I can't even see what she's doing."

Sommers considered for a moment. "As much as I'd like to make a joke about that, I won't."

Raine finally surrendered that smile. "Because you don't want me to feel bad or because you don't think it's true?"

"Oh, neither of those things," Sommers replied. "Because it would reflect badly on me as well."

Raine appreciated her honesty. He pointed back toward the festivities, and specifically the wandering caterers with their trays of libations. "Shall we mingle? I could use a drink."

"I couldn't agree more."

RAINE HAD ATTEMPTED several times to run into Thorne and start a conversation, but every time he spied her across the gallery, one or both of them was diverted by some third person needing their attention. Raine had lost count of the number of times he had given someone directions to the restrooms. But those were good problems to have. Despite the slow start, a steady stream of patrons filled the gallery and it appeared the evening might be a success after all.

Raine realized his optimism might have been a result of the champagne, but then again, so was the apparent success of the evening. Inhibitions were lowered and bids were raised. Many of the pieces had already reached their maximum recommended bid and were effectively sold, an exciting milestone for the young artists who had braved the second attempt at the gallery showing. There was one piece in particular Raine was interested in seeing whether it had received any bids. Any above his own, that was.

Veronica Kwon had been allowed even more wall space than at the first event. That was in part because there were fewer works competing for space. But it was also because she was a very talented artist. Finch and/or Thorne must have recognized that. Even Raine did.

He stepped up to the painting of the waves crashing on the night beach, its artist hovering nearby. The bid card was almost full. His initial bid, hastily scrawled out before the doors opened and while Kwon was engaged elsewhere, had been outdone by more than tenfold.

"Well, that's disappointing," he said, with a nod toward the painting.

Kwon turned and recognized him. "Oh, Dan. Hi. Are you feeling better?"

"I am," Raine confirmed. "Thank you again for your help

that night. Did you ever figure out who did that to me?"

Kwon's hesitation was all the answer Raine needed.

"I don't care who it was," Raine said. "I'm a lawyer. I don't call the police on people. I defend people from the police. Just do something terrible back to them for me, if you get the chance."

Kwon laughed lightly. "Okay. I can do that." Then she asked, "What's disappointing? Do you not like this painting after all?"

"No, I like it very much," Raine assured her. "Enough to bid on it. But it appears I've been outbid, and by a significant margin."

Kwon leaned forward and squinted at the bid card. "Oh wow. Yeah. Um, that's pretty cool."

Raine smiled. "It sure is. How are your other pieces doing?"

Kwon examined the bid card for her other four pieces. "Not as well as that one. But I do have a bid on one other painting. The one with the tree."

"Just my luck," Raine remarked, "to like the one everyone else likes."

"Yeah, well," Kwon shrugged, "that kind of happens. Everybody likes *Starry Night*, right?"

"Maybe I'll swing by at the end of the night," Raine said, "and see if I can grab one of the less universal pieces. I feel like it's the least I can do to repay you."

"Thanks," Kwon said. "And thanks for whatever you did to help organize this. I heard the gallery owner is getting sued by Hailey's parents and I heard you're his lawyer. That all kinda sucks, so it's nice to have something at least sorta good come out of it."

"You heard right," Raine admitted. "And yeah, there's a

lot of bad in the world. It's how I make my living. I don't mind helping other people make a living doing something good. Is this what you want to do for a living then?"

Another shrug from Kwon. "I would love that, but it's really hard to do just that. Most artists have to take a regular job to pay their bills. The trick is not having to work so much that you don't feel like creating anymore. I want to avoid that."

Raine was about to say, '*I'm sure you will*,' but he was not sure of any such thing. In fact, he supposed that was probably the norm. "Well, maybe you can use your money from *Beachy Night* to help fund future art."

Kwon frowned for a moment. She nodded at her painting. "It's not titled *Beachy Night*."

"Uh, right. I know. I was just making a play on *Starry Night*," Raine explained.

"Ah," Kwon replied.

"Yeah." It was time to move on. "Well, anyway. Thanks again and good luck."

"Thanks, Dan," Kwon replied. "And good luck to you too with your terrible job."

Raine smiled at the barb, but not because it wasn't true. He was about to take his leave when he finally found himself in the same room as Selina Thorne. She came gliding into the room, some woman Raine didn't know next to her, and seemed almost surprised to see anyone else in the room.

"Oh! Veronica, Daniel. What are you doing here?"

"I'm exhibiting my art?" Kwon tried.

"And I'm giving bad names to them," Raine added.

Thorne's eyebrows lowered as she considered what she had been told. Raine wondered how many of those free champagnes she'd had already.

"Yes, well, I am also exhibiting my art," Thorne said. "To this person here with me. What did you say your name was again?"

"Samantha," the woman answered.

"Yes, Samantha!" Thorne bellowed. "I was telling Samantha that I had one piece of my own that I decided to display, and she insisted on seeing it. So here we are. And there," she pointed at a painting on the far side of the room, "is my painting. Would you like to see it?"

"Absolutely," Raine answered. He wasn't about to say no to Thorne, but he was also genuinely interested to see more of what Thorne painted.

"What about you, Veronica?" Thorne prodded.

But Kwon turned her back to them and waved them off with a hand. "No, thanks. I've already seen it."

So, Raine, Thorne, and Samantha left Kwon to her own paintings and made their way across the room. Thorne's painting was modern art. A collection of geometric lines and shapes intersecting atop a background that tried to be both interesting and unobtrusive.

"What do you think?" Thorne asked.

"I love it!" Samantha enthused. "It's absolutely brilliant."

Thorne grinned broadly and turned to Raine. "What do you think?"

"It seems familiar," Raine said. That was the main feeling he was getting from it.

"Ah yes, well." Thorned tucked a strand of hair over her ear. "I suppose it's similar to the one you saw in my office."

"Sure, that makes sense," Raine agreed. "Well, I think it's great. I don't know a lot about art, especially modern art, but this one makes me think of a place that's safe and warm."

Thorne smiled. "What a nice thought. I'm so grateful both of you like it."

Raine was grateful he'd managed to think of something positive to say.

THE EVENING HAD ALMOST COME to a close. The champagne had almost run dry and final bids had been called. So, of course that was when things turned to shit.

"Dan!" Sommers rushed into the side room Raine was meandering through, gazing at the paintings for what seemed like the hundredth time that night while waiting for the gala to end. "You need to come out here."

"What's going on?"

"There are some very large, very dangerous-looking people here," Sommers explained, "and they're looking for Duncan."

Raine could guess who they were. "Where's Duncan?"

Sommers frowned slightly. "He's hiding in the ladies' room."

Raine nodded. "Great. So I'm supposed to talk to these guys for him?"

"Well, you are his lawyer," Sommers answered.

Not about his gambling debts, Raine thought, but he didn't say it out loud. He had his own reasons to engage with the party-crashers. Duncan couldn't afford for the gala to collapse again. Which meant Raine couldn't afford it either. He followed Sommers toward the main hall. She was remarkably fast in her high heels.

The men were not difficult to spot. In addition to being large, dressed in long black leather coats, and generally looking menacing, they were also being avoided by everyone else present. There was a semi-circle of people at the edges of the gallery, with the three of them at the center, their backs to the door, hands in their pockets, scowls on their faces.

Raine stepped out from the crowd and approached the unwelcome visitors. "Can I help you, gentlemen? I think you may be in the wrong place, or at least at the wrong time."

The shortest of the three men responded. It wasn't that he was short; he was shorter than his compatriots, but he was still as tall as Raine. It was just that the other two were enormous. "We're in the right place. And it's the right time. Duncan Finch owes me money and it's due today."

Raine considered his options. Physical force was out of the question. He was outnumbered and outsized. Calling the police wasn't likely a legitimate threat. The men were obviously comfortable operating on the other side of the law, and as he'd told Kwon, he wasn't on Team Thin Blue Line. That left wits and words. His forte.

"I think you're in luck then, sir," he said. "The day isn't quite over and the event you've walked into is designed to secure the funds you're owed. May I suggest returning in approximately two hours? I'm sure Mr. Finch will be happy to settle his debt with you as soon as possible."

The man stared at Raine for several seconds. He had a puffy face, with ruddy, acne-scarred cheeks and thin lips. His eyes were dark and dull. "Who the fuck are you?"

"I'm Mr. Finch's attorney," Raine responded. "I'm authorized to speak on his behalf."

"I want to see Finch now," the man demanded. "I want to make sure he hasn't skipped town."

"I can assure you," Raine said, "Mr. Finch is very close by

and eager to conclude his business relationship with you."

The man seemed unimpressed. Raine supposed he couldn't blame him. He was a man who broke other people's hands. Politeness wasn't really his language. So, Raine tried a different tongue.

"Listen," he lowered his voice and gestured for the man to take a step away from his companions so they could speak semi-privately, "I know you broke Finch's hand. I was actually there. Heard the whole thing. And I understand why. There are harsh realities to these sorts of business arrangements and sometimes people need to be reminded what their priorities need to be. But here's the thing. Breaking someone's hand is assault in the second degree. Now, I know that's only a Level Four offense, but you know it only takes a couple of priors to get to a twelve-month sentence and you're off to state prison."

He put an arm around the man's shoulder. "What I'm saying is, you look like the sort of person who has probably broken a lot of people's bones, and I bet at least one of those prior encounters led to criminal charges. Which means, if the police were contacted about what happened to Mr. Finch, you would be facing the very real possibility of going to prison for at least a year."

Raine removed his arm and clasped his hands together thoughtfully. "Now, don't get me wrong. I'm sure you could do a year in prison standing on your head. Hell, you'd probably be in charge of your block by the end of the first week. But what's your boss supposed to do while you're sitting in a prison on the other side of the state? I mean, it's obvious you work for someone else, and it's obvious that person expects results. He's not going to just put his entire business on hold until you get out again, right? No, of course not. He's going to replace you. Not with these two goons. They have their roles. They're not getting promoted. But there's somebody who wants your job. Someone your boss already has been thinking about. You probably already know who it'll be, right? So, someone calls the police, reports your little assault two, and the next thing you know, you're off to Walla Walla, and when you get out, you're out of a job and it's back to stealing mail and selling pills again."

Raine gestured around at the gallery and its assembled, if nervous, guests. "Or, you let us finish what we need to do to get your money, you come back in two hours to get it, and everybody is happy, except that fucker who wants to steal your job. So, whattaya say? You and the boys go grab a beer up the street and we'll see you in two hours. Deal?"

The man had remained silent during Raine's pitch. That meant he was listening. He didn't dismiss it immediately upon Raine's conclusion. That meant he was thinking. Finally, he held up his index and middle fingers. "Two hours. Finch better have my money or I'm going to break your hand, and maybe more. Do we understand each other?"

"We do," Raine confirmed.

The man grunted in reply, then motioned for his henchmen to follow him out the doors.

Raine waited a few moments, then turned around to address the crowd. "Wrong party," he announced. "They were looking for the knife convention up the street. Please, return to whatever you were doing. The time for bidding is almost over and it will soon be time to collect your works of art."

And for Finch to collect the money. He hoped Finch was set up for electronic payments. They weren't going to be able to cash any checks at that hour.

Sommers rushed up to him. "What did you say to make them leave?"

Raine stood up a little bit taller. "I told him if he didn't leave I'd kick his ass in front of his buddies and these people here, so if he didn't want to be humiliated, he'd better get the fuck out of here."

"No, seriously. What did you say?"

Raine laughed a bit. "I told him to come back in two hours and Finch would have the money, and I explained why that was in his long-term financial interests."

"Two hours?" Sommers exclaimed. "Duncan better be set up for—"

"Electronic payments, yes," Raine agreed. "We should probably start telling people that's the preferred method of payment. You should go and get his account info."

"Why me?" Sommers questioned.

"Because he's hiding in the ladies' room."

Sommers sighed. "Right."

AN HOUR LATER, the payments were collected, the patrons and students had departed, and Raine and Sommers found themselves sitting in the front gallery along with Finch and Thorne.

"I declare this evening a success," Thorne said. "My students got their evening in the limelight, without being marred by tragedy. And we raised a respectable amount for both the school and Duncan's legal fees."

She raised her glass of champagne, but only Sommers followed suit.

"What's wrong, Duncan?" Thorne asked. "Daniel? Is

there something I missed?"

Raine realized he hadn't ever mentioned Finch's injury or the reasons behind it to Thorne. Then again, that was really Finch's story to tell.

"Is there going to be anything left over to cover my fees?" Raine suspected he knew the answer.

"Maybe," Finch tried. "Or maybe not. Probably not. Not all of it anyway."

Raine pinched the bridge of his nose and shook his head. "I'm glad you're not going to get your other hand broken, Duncan, but I have to be honest. This entire case has been an absolute disaster. Dead art students, broken bones, spiked drinks. I'm afraid to ask what's next."

"Spiked drinks?" Sommers asked, inspecting her own flute of champagne.

"Long story." Raine waved off the inquiry. "The point is, come Monday, you and I are going to have a long talk about the case and whether I can continue to represent you. I'm not greedy, but I'm not free either. Trial is right around the corner. Things are about to get even more expensive."

Finch nodded along. "I think I know how to make it work. I really want you to stay on the case. I don't want to change horses midstream."

Raine was glad to hear that, if also dubious. He decided he didn't want to think about finances anymore that night. "Let's not talk business. Tonight should be about the Cascadia Art School and The Finch Gallery." He raised his glass. "Here's to, um...?" He looked to Sommers.

"Art?" she suggested.

"Yes, art," Raine agreed. "Here's to art." He smiled at Thorne. "And the artists who create it."

Thorne returned the smile but looked away.

Maybe getting out of the case wouldn't be the worst thing, Raine thought. He also thought he really needed to use the bathroom. "Now, if you'll excuse me for a moment, I need to use the facilities."

He set his drink down, then remembered the last time he did that and decided to drain it before crossing to the hallway to the restrooms. The men's room was tucked around the corner just past the women's room where Hailey Parker's body had been found. He was tempted to peek inside to make sure they didn't have another dead art student, but decided better of it. No good would come out of peeking into women's restrooms.

The men's room also appeared to be free of any dead bodies. Although, upon inspection, it was also free of toilet paper, in any of the stalls.

"It's always something," he muttered to himself.

He had noticed the caterers going to a supply closet at the far side of the kitchen across the hall. Maybe that was where Finch stored the extra toilet paper. Raine really didn't want to go back out to the group and announce why he needed Finch to tell him where the toilet paper was. He crossed the hall and entered the kitchen. It was an absolute mess. Apparently the price of the caterer didn't cover cleanup. The storage closet was past the sink and prep counter, both filled with dirty glasses and empty bottles. He wondered whether there might be another bottle of champagne in the storage closet too. They had an hour to kill before Finch's loan shark returned.

Upon opening the door, Raine did not see either toilet paper or champagne. But that was because his eyes were filled with the scene of Veronica Kwon, dead on the floor, her throat slit from ear to ear.

19

"Well, fuck," Raine hissed.

He didn't really know Veronica Kwon, a night at her apartment notwithstanding. But she had been kind to him. He had liked her.

The scene was reminiscent of Hailey Parker's death, despite the variance in location and method of death. Instead of a gun lying on the floor a few inches from the dead girl's hand, it was a box cutter. The pool of blood was also bigger. Parker's heart had been pierced and immediately stopped beating. Kwon's heart kept pumping blood out of her neck until it ran dry.

He wanted to spend more time inspecting the scene, but the hair on the back of his neck was starting to stand up. This one was definitely a murder, and a murder meant there was a murderer. It wasn't safe to be off on his own, especially close to the body, where the murderer might still be hiding. Raine backed slowly out of the storage closet and closed the door.

Raine ran to the main hall and called out to the others. "Rebecca! Selina! Duncan! Come quick!"

"What is it, Dan?" Sommers called out.

"Murder!" Raine answered.

There was a pause as the others processed what Raine had just said.

"Did you say murder?" Sommers asked for all of them.

"Yes," Raine confirmed. He waved frantically for them to come over. "Hurry!"

Sommers didn't need any further prompting, but Finch let out a high-pitched moan and appeared to faint.

"Go on, you two," Thorne said. "I'll revive Duncan and we'll be right there."

Raine wasn't so sure, but he was glad for Sommers's presence at least.

"Who is it?" she asked as she ran up to him.

"Veronica Kwon." He turned and led her back to the body at a jog.

"Who's that?"

"She's an art student," Raine answered. "I spent a night at her apartment."

"Whoa, what?" Sommers responded. "You fucked the murder victim?"

Raine pulled up to a walk as they reached the kitchen and he stared at her for a moment. "Do you even realize how bad that sounds, in how many ways? No, I didn't sleep with her. It's a long story."

"A lot of those tonight," Sommers recalled.

"Same story," Raine told her. "Now, hush. The body is in the storage closet."

Raine half-expected it to be missing, the blood stain either left behind to confirm what he'd seen or mysteriously cleaned up to make him look crazy in front of the others. But nothing so dramatic. Veronica Kwon was still there, and she was still dead.

"Holy crap," Sommers gasped. She covered her face with her hands. The small room was stuffy with the smell of blood and death.

Raine agreed with the sentiment, but he didn't respond. Instead, he took the opportunity to scan the scene for anything that might indicate what had happened, or better yet, why.

"Shouldn't we call the cops?" Sommers suggested.

Raine had forgotten about that. "Oh yeah. I guess we should."

"I'll do it," Sommers volunteered.

Raine was glad for that. He wanted to continue his inspection of the scene. But it only took a few moments to realize there wasn't anything of obvious value. The killer had not in fact dropped his wallet, or left behind a telltale fake fingernail. There was just a dead woman and a whole lot of blood. Raine could hear Sommers giving the 911 operator the address of the gallery. The cops would be there within minutes. He stepped back and took out his phone, but not to call 911.

"You're taking pictures?" Sommers chastised after she hung up and returned to where Raine was standing.

"The cops are going to lock this place down as soon as they get here," Raine explained. "We'll never get this close again and I don't want to have overlooked something that could help Duncan."

"You think this helps Duncan?" Sommers questioned. "The guy can't throw an event without someone dying."

"Yes, I think this helps Duncan," Raine answered. "This

one is definitely a murder. That means the first one may have been a murder too after all. It should be enough to get that lazy ass detective to reopen the investigation. And no matter what, the jury will hear about this. Amanda Stone may be a cold-blooded litigation strategist, but I'd like to hear her explain why Hailey Parker's death was so certainly a suicide when her best friend was murdered under similar circumstances so soon afterward."

"I guess that makes sense," Sommers allowed.

"And if the cops actually catch the killer?" Raine imagined. "Well, then the case will be dismissed. We win and Duncan won't owe me any more money after all."

THE POLICE ARRIVED EVEN FASTER than Raine had expected. He barely managed to finish photographing the scene before a squad of patrol officers burst into the kitchen and rousted him and Sommers out and back into the main hall. Raine found that encouraging. What he found less encouraging occurred about fifteen minutes later when the detective arrived. It was Crenshaw again.

"Detective Crenshaw!" he called out across the lobby. He was prevented from going over to her by a very large uniformed officer whose single task was preventing Raine and the others from leaving until the detective authorized it. At least they were handling it like a murder scene this time. "Detective, it's Daniel Raine. The attorney. I'm the one who found the body."

Crenshaw stopped her march toward the kitchen long enough to stare at Raine for a few seconds. "Aren't you that delivery guy from Mickey's?"

Raine hung his head.

"I'll be with you when I'm ready to talk with you, sir," Crenshaw told him. "In the meantime, extra bacon, no citrus."

Raine returned to his seat with the others.

"What the hell was that all about?" Sommers asked him.

"Long story," Raine replied.

"The same long story, or a different long story?" Sommers inquired.

"Different long story," Raine answered. "Although it looks like we might have time for both of them tonight."

The only good part of being stuck inside the gallery while the police sealed it off was that the puffy-faced hand-breaker couldn't come in to collect his debt from Finch. It was a small respite, they knew. Finch needed to be ready for a visit from him in the morning, but it allowed him one more night without the threat of physical violence. Well, to himself anyway. There had been plenty of physical violence in his kitchen.

By the time Crenshaw was finally ready to talk with them, more than two hours had passed. Thorne had fallen asleep on a bench, having fetched her coat and balled it up into a pillow. Sommers appeared to be doing email and other work on her phone the entire time. She was always very industrious. Finch spent the entire two hours sitting in a tight ball on the floor and rocking back and forth. And Raine just sat on a bench against the wall, leaned his head back, closed his eyes, and let his mind wander wherever it wanted. Some of the usual destinations popped up—Nat, the kids, that weird hot dog stand outside the hotel on their honeymoon in Hawaii—but there were new ones as well. The Quarry club, Kwon's apartment, Sommers's standing table at the yacht club she belonged to. It had been a strange night.

"Well, Mr. Finch," Crenshaw belted out as she jarred the four of them from their thoughts and dreams, "you seem to be one very unlucky guy. Remind me not to come to your gallery when I'm depressed."

Raine's heart sank. "You don't think this is also—"

"A suicide," Crenshaw finished the sentence. "Yes, sir. It's looking that way."

Raine blinked at her for several seconds. "Her throat was slit. Like, all the way across."

Crenshaw nodded. "Sure was. But that doesn't mean it wasn't suicide. You don't die from the cut, you die from bleeding out after the cut. It would hurt, but you could definitely slit your own throat. I think that even used to be a ritual method of self-sacrifice in some cultures."

"I'm sure you're wrong," Raine said.

"About the ritual self-sacrifice?" Crenshaw responded. "Maybe. I don't know. But I feel like I heard that somewhere along the way."

"No, not that," Raine answered. "Well, that too, probably. But no. You're wrong about Veronica's death. That was a murder."

"Veronica?" Crenshaw repeated back. "So, you were on a first-name basis with her?"

"Long story," Sommers put in.

Raine glared at her.

"I'm sure," Crenshaw replied. "But I'll have to hear it some other time. You all are free to go."

"Don't you want to take statements from us?" Raine suggested.

"For a suicide?" Crenshaw scoffed. "No. No need for that."

"But it wasn't a suicide," Raine insisted. "It was a murder."

"Agree to disagree," Crenshaw replied. "Except it doesn't matter that you disagree. I'm the detective. I get to make that call."

"And what are you basing that call on?" Raine demanded. He stood up and stepped to the detective. "How much paperwork you have to do for a murder versus a suicide?"

Cops didn't like being stepped to. They really didn't like it when someone stepped to one of their superiors. The large officer who had been assigned to guard them and another officer with a barrel chest and thick forearms rushed up to him.

"No, no. Calm down, fellas," Crenshaw instructed. "Mr. Raine isn't going to do anything stupid. He's a lawyer. The last thing he would do is assault a police officer."

It was definitely not the last thing Raine would do, but he wasn't about to do it then.

"Don't worry, Mr. Raine," Crenshaw continued. "I'll withhold my final verdict until after I get the autopsy report. But I'll go ahead and tell you that there were no signs of a struggle. If someone tried to slice my throat open, you can bet there'd be furniture turned over and cuts all over my hands from grabbing at the blade. I don't just make this stuff up, you know. I've seen a lot of deaths over the years, sir, and I've gotten pretty good at being able to tell which ones are murder, and which ones are self-inflicted."

"And I bet you got every single one of them right," Raine said, "since you're the one who decides if you're right."

Crenshaw frowned, but didn't reply. Instead, she turned to walk away. "Escort these lovely people out of the building, officers," she commanded over her shoulder. "They're done here."

20

Raine knew better than to try to convince Detective Crenshaw to change her mind. It wouldn't work. And after he calmed down, Raine realized it didn't matter anyway. He could still argue to the jury that Veronica Kwon's death was evidence of something larger at play. Larger than Duncan Finch anyway. Once the jury met Finch, they shouldn't have too much trouble believing that.

For his part, Finch advised Raine that he had paid off his debts to the puffy-faced man. Raine wasn't sure whether to believe him, but decided to do so because it allowed him to close that chapter of his relationship with Finch. There had been a little bit left over from Finch's cut of the gala proceeds to pay Raine at least for the work he had done to that point. The retainer was still empty and there was still a lot of work to do, but Raine decided to be patient. Finch was good for the money, even without the threat of breaking his hand, and the best way to make sure he had sufficient funds to pay him was to win the trial.

There was only one hurdle left between them and that

trial: Stone's deposition of Finch. A deposition was basically a dry run of the questioning of the witness at trial. The one piece of advice every trial attorney knew was, 'Never ask a question you don't already know the answer to.' Depositions helped with that by giving each attorney an opportunity to question the witness, under oath, prior to questioning them again in front of the jury at trial. It also helped what was called the defending attorney—that is, the attorney who represented the witness being deposed. The deposition provided a sneak preview of the questioning to come at trial, and even an insight into the other side's trial strategy.

Raine didn't mind giving Finch a little practice at being grilled by Stone. And there was nothing he could do about it anyway. Stone was entitled to depose Finch, and the date and time she had dictated actually worked for Raine's schedule.

He met Finch at the offices of Churchill, Walmer, and Pickwick on the 34th floor of the Columbia Center. It was close enough from his office to walk, and he didn't want to carpool with a client anyway. That was just awkward. Absent the lawsuit, the two of them likely never would have crossed paths again after what turned out to be the first exhibition.

"Are you ready?" Raine asked Finch once they were both in the lobby. They had spent some time to prepare for the deposition, but it didn't take that long to say, 'Tell the truth.' It wasn't some complex commercial litigation case with hidden assets and secret offshore accounts. Hailey Parker's death wasn't Finch's fault. He just needed to remember that and work it into as many responses as possible.

"No," Finch answered with a nervous laugh. "But I don't suppose that matters, does it?"

"Not really," Raine agreed. "Just remember what I told

you. Answer the question posed, but only the question posed. Don't volunteer any information they don't ask about. And above all else..."

"Tell the truth," Finch finished the sentence.

"Tell the truth," Raine repeated. "Follow those rules and we'll be done by dinner time."

Finch frowned and checked the time. "It's nine in the morning."

Raine nodded. "Yeah, these can take a while. Don't worry though. They probably have snacks."

Finch's expression dropped, but before he could say anything, some lower-level employee appeared in the lobby. "Ms. Stone is ready for you now," the woman informed them. She looked like she might be an attorney, judging by her dark suit and professional hairstyle. But then again, the firm might require all of its employees to dress like that. Large corporate law firms were not known for their embrace of individual expression.

Raine and Finch stood up and followed the woman into the interior of the firm's offices. Raine was interested to see how the other half lived, but unfortunately for him, they were taken directly to a conference room only some ten feet from the door to the lobby. The woman gestured for them to go inside. Raine directed Finch to enter first, then followed before the woman closed the door behind them.

The first thing Raine noticed was the view. Thirty-four stories up, everything looked pretty amazing, but the conference room faced west, so they had an unobstructed view of the waterfront, Elliott Bay, and the Olympic Mountains beyond. The second thing Raine noticed was that Stone was alone in the conference room.

"Where's the court reporter?" Raine asked. They would

need a court reporter to swear Finch in under oath and produce a verbatim transcript of the deposition.

"There's no court reporter," Stone answered. She was seated at the far end of the conference table, and had not stood up when Raine and Finch entered. "There will be no deposition today."

"What?" Raine was shocked.

"Thank goodness!" Finch exclaimed.

"Why no deposition?" Raine asked. "And why didn't you tell us before we came all the way over here?"

Stone finally stood up. She picked up a document off the conference table and handed it to Raine. "This is why. To both of your questions."

Raine looked at the paper. It was a pleading. It was titled, 'Amended Complaint.' "What are you amending? Is my client responsible for the sinking of the Titanic now too? Global warming? The Mariners never making it to a World Series?"

"Read the caption," Stone directed.

He did. "Oh."

"What?" Finch asked, his relief at the deposition being canceled quickly replaced with trepidation of whatever was transpiring between the attorneys via the document in Raine's hand.

"The case is now not just *Mark and Susan Parker versus Duncan Finch*," Raine explained. "It's *Mark and Susan Parker and Philip and Cynthia Kwon versus Duncan Finch*."

"I'm being sued by her parents too now?" Finch shrieked. He dropped into one of the chairs at the conference table. "Oh my God. I think I'm going to faint."

Raine held up the pleading. "Wow, Amanda. Just wow. Do you actually have someone assigned to chase ambulances to the hospital? Or I guess in this case it would be chasing the hearse to the morgue, but you understand what I mean. Did you actually call Veronica's parents and ask them to join the lawsuit? I mean, we both know that's unethical, but I feel like a big firm like this sees ethical violations as a cost of doing business."

"I don't discuss how our firm is retained, Mr. Raine," Stone replied. "I can simply tell you that the Kwons were heartbroken to lose their daughter, and outraged when they learned that this had happened before."

"Sure, sure, whatever." Raine tossed the amended complaint on the conference room table. "So, what's the theory of liability for the second alleged suicide? Did my client not say hello to her when she arrived to hang her work in his gallery, *again*, for *free*? Were the *hors d'oeuvres* too salty? Maybe the lighting wasn't flattering to her good side? I know they ran out of toilet paper at one point."

"You can make all the jokes you want, Mr. Raine," Stone responded. "We will be adding the Kwons as plaintiffs in this case. As a result, I realize you will need a continuance of the trial to prepare for—"

"No, fuck that." Raine waved a hand at her. "I don't need a continuance. I'm ready. Let's try this case. The facts are pretty much uncontested, right? Dead girl number one, dead girl number two. You and I argue over whose fault it is, and the jury decides. I don't need extra time to prepare for you making your case even more obviously a craven grab for money at the expense, not just of my client, but the mental well-being of your own clients. Both sets now, I guess."

"Do not presume to tell me how best to care for my clients," Stone growled at him.

"And don't presume I want a continuance when the thing

I want most is to get this case in front of a jury." He gestured at the otherwise empty conference room. "I didn't tell you to call off the court reporter. That was your decision. It sounds to me like you've canceled your deposition of my client. Accordingly, we will be taking our leave now. See you at the readiness hearing."

"If you don't ask for a continuance at the readiness hearing, we will," Stone called out as Raine headed for the exit.

"And I will object," Raine replied. "See you in court, Stone."

21

The readiness hearing was supposed to be a perfunctory check-in with the judge on the Friday before trial started the following Monday. It was not supposed to become a hearing on a contested motion to amend the complaint and continue the trial. But then, two people weren't supposed to kill themselves and/or get murdered at an art gallery in downtown Seattle. Life could be unpredictable.

Raine eschewed any conversation with Stone as they waited for the judge. No small talk, no trash talk, not even last-minute negotiations. Just two lawyers waiting for the battle to commence, their unwitting clients seated ignorantly next to them. Raine had been blunt with Finch, perhaps even rude. His instructions were, "Do not talk to me. At all. About anything. I need to concentrate, and not on you. Do you understand?" Finch assured him that he did.

When the judge came out at just after 1:00 p.m., she was experienced enough to feel that something was amiss. The readiness hearing was the last chance to be relatively relaxed in court before spending every subsequent day in front of a jury scrutinizing your every move. The readiness hearing was not for attorneys to be already seated at the counsel tables, expressions serious, body language tense, ready for battle.

"All rise!" the bailiff began the ceremonial call. "The King County Superior Court is now—"

"Nuh, uh, uh," Judge Castro hushed her bailiff. She stood above the litigants and put her hands on her hips. "What's going on? Is there a problem about Monday? Does somebody have a dentist appointment or something? We can start late, if that's what it is."

"That is not what it is, Your Honor," Raine responded. But he didn't elucidate. He was ready for trial. It was Stone who was causing the problems.

"What is it then?" Castro asked. She turned to the other table. "Ms. Stone?"

"Thank you, Your Honor," Stone led with deference. "My law firm has been retained by another set of parents who wish to join the lawsuit against Mr. Finch and his gallery. We are seeking to amend our complaint and then we expect the Court will continue the trial to a new date later in the year."

The judge nodded along to the explanation before turning back to Raine. "Is that your understanding, Mr. Raine? And will you be requesting a continuance to prepare to defend against the claims from additional plaintiffs?"

"It is my understanding that Ms. Stone has found additional clients to sue Mr. Finch," Raine answered. "I do not want a continuance. I am ready for trial, even with these new plaintiffs."

"Have you conducted any investigation," Judge Castro

asked, "into the claims being brought by these new plaintiffs?"

"I discovered the body," Raine answered, "if that's what you mean, Your Honor."

"Body?" Castro questioned. "You discovered Hailey Parker's body?"

"I discovered Veronica Kwon's body, Your Honor," Raine explained.

The judge's eyes narrowed and she finally sat down. "Who is Veronica Kwon?"

"She is another student at the Cascadia Art School," Stone answered, "who took her life after a second and even more egregiously upsetting art exhibition at the defendant's gallery. One designed to profit off the memory of Hailey Parker but which only served to extinguish another young life."

Castro squinted down at the lawyers. "There was another exhibition? There was another suicide?"

"Yes," Raine answered, "and maybe."

Judge Castro nodded for several seconds. "Okay. Let me see if I have this straight. There was an exhibition of student art at the defendant's gallery, however long ago. That night, Hailey Parker committed suicide. Her parents are suing the defendant, alleging he was responsible for her decision to kill herself. Then, sometime since we last saw each other, there was another exhibition, again of student art, again at the defendant's gallery. This time another student committed suicide—maybe, says Mr. Raine—but in any event, this second woman's parents also want to sue the defendant, asserting the same or similar reasons. Do I have that pretty much right?"

"Yes, Your Honor," Stone replied.

"Yes, Your Honor," Raine agreed.

"And Mr. Raine," the judge continued, "you don't want to continue the trial scheduled to begin in three days, even though there would be this entire new aspect of the case?"

"I do not want to continue the trial, Your Honor," Raine answered. "I understand what Ms. Stone is arguing and I am prepared to meet it as to both sets of plaintiffs."

Castro put a hand to her chin and leaned back, nodding, as she considered the situation.

"And if I may, Your Honor," Raine continued, "just as Mr. Finch never asked to be sued by the Parkers, he also never asked to be sued by the Kwons. It is the plaintiffs, through Ms. Stone, who made the decision to file this lawsuit. Mr. Finch can't prevent them from suing him, but he can be ready to defend himself. And we are ready, Your Honor."

It was all well and good to praise yourself, Raine knew, but real persuasion often lay in attacking the opponent.

"This appears to be nothing more than a delay tactic orchestrated by Ms. Stone," he continued. "We appeared as directed for Ms. Stone's deposition of Mr. Finch, but when we arrived, she had already canceled the court reporter and handed me a copy of her amended complaint, as if that explained why she chose not to go forward with the deposition. It is Ms. Stone who wants the delay, Your Honor, not me, and certainly not my client. If Ms. Stone is not prepared to begin trial on Monday, then all she has to do is dismiss her complaint and terminate the litigation. But if she is not prepared to do that, then she should be prepared to start trial on Monday. I certainly am."

Judge Castro smiled. "Okay, I see what's happened. Ms. Stone made a calculation that additional plaintiffs would require a delay in the trial. She made a decision that didn't come without some risk. Mr. Raine now wants to make her pay for that risk. If we proceed on Monday, we do so without the plaintiffs' attorney ever having deposed the defendant."

Raine resisted the urge to add anything to the judge's summary of how they had gotten to where they were. Stone should have resisted her own urge to do the same.

"I canceled the court reporter because I wasn't ready to depose the defendant," she complained. "There has been an entire new death, Your Honor. I would like to be prepared for that before proceeding with a deposition of the defendant."

"I'm sure you would, Ms. Stone," the judge replied, "but sometimes things don't work out like we want them to. Mr. Raine appears to be correct. You chose to add new plaintiffs to this suit and you chose to cancel your opportunity to depose your opponent. Why should the trial be delayed over Mr. Finch's objection if the delay is your fault and not his?"

"I hardly think you can describe the situation as being my fault, Your Honor," Stone protested.

"I would disagree," the judge interjected. "You made decisions on how to proceed with a lawsuit you filed. Mr. Raine says he's ready to go despite those decisions of yours. We have literally hundreds of cases backed up, waiting for a courtroom. If you filed a lawsuit and the defendant says he's ready for trial, why shouldn't you have to choose between conducting that trial or dismissing your suit?"

"Why?" Stone repeated. "I'll tell you why, Your Honor. Justice, that's why. My clients deserve their day in court and they deserve justice. But they also deserve to have an attorney who is as prepared as humanly possible to fight for them. There is a lot left to do before this case is ready to proceed to trial."

"And yet," the judge pointed out, "Mr. Raine says he is ready for trial. Are you ready for trial, Mr. Raine?"

"Yes, Your Honor," Raine confirmed. "I am ready for trial."

Castro gestured at Raine and Finch. "See? They're ready. You sued them and they're ready for trial. You seem to have caused your own reasons for not being ready."

Stone took a moment to compose herself. Raine knew being disrespectful, let alone angry, with a judge was unlikely to persuade the judge to side with you. Stone undoubtedly knew that as well. "Your Honor—"

"Eh, I've heard enough," the judge interrupted. "I am going to allow the filing of the amended complaint and the addition of the new plaintiffs to the lawsuit. Then I am going to deny what is essentially the plaintiffs' request for a continuance of the trial. Mr. Raine says he's ready. I guess we'll see if that's true. Trial is confirmed for Monday. I will see everyone then."

She banged her gavel for good measure and stood up.

"All rise!" the bailiff called out. "Court is at recess."

Finch leaned over and whispered to Raine. "Can I talk to you now?"

Raine smiled slightly. He appreciated his client's willingness to do as he was told. "Yes, you can talk to me."

"Did we win?" Finch asked.

Raine looked over at Stone, struggling to explain the judge's ruling to her clients, then back to his own client. "It's too soon to tell."

22

Raine headed back to his office, feeling pleased with his victory but nevertheless trepidatious about the upcoming trial. Be careful what you wish for, he thought. He had managed to force Stone into the trial with less preparation than she wanted, but he was in the same boat. His advantage, if he had one, was that he was familiar with that boat. Solo practitioners, especially solo practitioners who also handled criminal cases, were used to relying on their instincts and shooting from the hip. Real trial attorneys learned to get into the ring and start swinging, even if they weren't quite ready for the bell. On the other hand, so-called 'litigation' attorneys at big corporate law firms were used to billing their clients a small fortune while they tried to dot every i and cross every t before setting foot in the courtroom.

It was easier for Raine as well because he was defending the case. He didn't have to prove anything. The burden was on Stone to establish that Finch had been responsible for Hailey Parker's decision to kill herself. And Veronica Kwon's alleged decision to do the same. That was a tall order. Raine could sit back, look for weak spots in Stone's presentation, then strike at the gaps in her armor.

That was a lot of metaphors for one walk back to his office from the courthouse. When he got there, he immediately gave Laura the rest of the afternoon off and retired to his office. The case having been confirmed for Monday, Raine considered himself to be officially 'in trial.' Everything else could, and should, wait. His plan was to pour himself a bourbon on the rocks and nurse it over the remainder of the afternoon while he sketched out questions for jury selection and the outlines of his opening statement. He would end the day with a thoughtful reflection on the nature of the justice system and his role in it, followed by a professionally responsible good night's sleep.

His plans lasted about twenty minutes. Then Sommers burst through his front door and directly into his office.

"It was Caleb!" she shouted. "It was fucking Caleb Marquardt!"

Raine looked up at his unexpected guest. "What?"

"Caleb!" Sommers repeated. "He's the buyer. All those shell corporations? Those were him. CNM Investments? Caleb N. Marquardt. MarQet Capital? It's a play on Marquardt. Shiboo, Incorporated? I don't know, probably his damn dog."

"Are you sure?" Raine asked. "How did you find out?"

"I talked with my contacts again," Sommers explained. "One of them, Randy Witherspoon—he was the seller's agent on the sale of the bookstore. He told me everything went through that damn law firm. But then he remembered seeing someone, who might have been the buyer, waiting outside while they went over the final paperwork. He called me to tell me. He wasn't sure it really was the buyer, and not just some guy leaning against a Tesla right outside his window at the same time they were signing the docs. But when he described him, I was sure. Very tall, expensive clothes, short curly red hair."

"That does sound like Marquardt," Raine concurred.

"Exactly," Sommers said. "I still can't get behind the public corporate documents to confirm, but I'm sure it's Caleb. It has to be. We need to confront him and make him confess."

Raine considered the information, and its impact. There was nothing illegal about what Marquardt had done. Not obviously so, anyway. It was certainly shady not to mention it to people he pretended to be friends with, but Raine was unlikely to be able to prove it was anything other than a savvy businessman taking advantage of a fortuitous situation. And as much satisfaction it might give Sommers to daylight Marquardt's deception, Raine's job was to defend Finch against the lawsuit brought by Amanda Stone on behalf of the Parkers and Kwons.

"No," he replied.

"No?" Sommers scoffed.

"Not yet," Raine clarified.

"Why not?" Sommers demanded.

"Because it doesn't help Duncan," Raine answered. "No one knows except you and me. If we confront Marquardt now, that will just give him time to come up with some explanation. And remember, his lawyers are Churchill, Walmer, and Pickwick. Stone already knows this, but she doesn't know we know. No, our best strategy is to keep this hidden until we're ready to use it at trial."

Sommers crossed her arms, but didn't argue. "An ambush, huh? I have to admit, I like the sound of that."

"Thanks," Raine said. "But this does change the entire defense."

"How?"

"I was going to argue that the entire case was a misguided effort by grieving parents," Raine explained. "I mean, I can hardly attack a couple who had lost their daughter. But the best stories have a bad guy, and now we have one."

"Caleb," Sommers practically spat out the name.

Raine shook his head. "Not Caleb. Stone. All of Churchill, Walmer, and Pickwick. They didn't get hired by grieving parents. They sought out a plaintiff to drive down the price of the gallery for the financial benefit of one of their other, long-standing clients."

Sommers nodded. "I like that. Make the lawyers the bad guys. That will work."

"Of course it will." Raine grinned. "Everybody hates lawyers."

23

M onday morning arrived, as Monday mornings were wont to do, and Raine made his way to the courthouse to meet his client outside of Judge Castro's courtroom. Finch was dressed more conservatively than Raine had ever seen. The suit was still tailored at the height of some fashion Raine wasn't privy to, but it was black, and his tie was a muted burgundy. Raine appreciated the effort. They were about to meet the jury for the first time. No matter what either of them wore after that day, the jury would always remember their first impression of them.

Amanda Stone knew that as well. She arrived just after Raine, her own four clients trailing like groupies. They all looked the model of successful, loving parents, and Stone looked like the top litigator in the state. Or at least that she thought she was.

"Mr. Raine," she greeted him formally as she reached past him for the courtroom door. "I hope you're as ready as you claimed to be on Friday. I certainly am."

"You're as prepared as you said you were on Friday?" Raine asked. "So, you're not ready at all?"

Raine knew the Parkers and Kwons could hear him. And he knew Stone knew that too. Planting a seed of doubt in the minds of the opposing party was Trial 101. He grinned at his own comment. He was looking forward to the game. Stone, for her perfect suit and hair, seemed less excited by the prospect of the trial. But she knew enough not to expose her clients to any further undermining quips by Raine.

"Come inside with me, folks," she directed to her clients. "We should get set up before the judge comes out."

As the door was closing behind them, Finch asked, "Don't we need to set up too?"

"There are five of them and only three chairs at each table," Raine explained. "We're fine."

"Is Rebecca coming too?" Finch asked, thinking of their third chair.

Raine shook his head. "No, this is lawyer time, not amateur investigator time. Rebecca can't take off weeks from her real estate job to sit and watch me and Stone trade off asking questions of anyone even remotely related to the death of those two women."

Finch frowned. "I suppose that makes sense."

"But don't worry, Duncan." Raine put a reassuring hand on his shoulder. "She's still working on the case while we're stuck in here. In fact, her work might be the key to turning the entire case in our favor."

Finch's expression lifted. "That's good. I'm glad she's on our team."

Raine smiled. "Me too. Now, let's get in there and fight like hell."

IN TRUTH, the fighting, like hell or otherwise, was actually several days away. First, they had to go over the rules. Then they had to pick the referees. It was only after those things were accomplished that anyone could throw any metaphorical punches, and even then they were delivered one at a time, alternating between the lawyers.

Judge Castro emerged from her chambers promptly at 9:00 a.m.

The bailiff called the courtroom to order. "All rise! The King County Superior Court is now in session, The Honorable Jennifer Castro presiding."

Everyone in the courtroom stood as directed, but it was a small crowd. Just the lawyers and the clients, seven in all. Anyone connected to the case or the parties was a potential witness and witnesses weren't allowed in the courtroom except during their testimony, lest they be tempted to change their story based on what they heard. Anyone not connected to the case or the parties didn't care about that particular lawsuit. For Duncan Finch, the Parkers, and the Kwons, the case was the most important thing in their lives. As far as everyone else in Seattle, no one cared.

"Are the parties ready on the matter of *Mark and Susan Parker and Philip and Cynthia Kwon versus Duncan Finch and The Finch Gallery*?" Judge Castro began the proceedings with the standard first question. Despite appearances, it was not an invitation to relitigate the issue of a continuance. The only acceptable delay at that point would be if someone needed to use the bathroom before they started picking the jury.

"The plaintiffs are ready, Your Honor," Stone stood to answer the judge.

Lawyers always stood to address a judge. And the plaintiff's lawyer always answered first; it was their fault everyone was there in the first place.

"The defendant is also ready, Your Honor," Raine stood and confirmed.

"Good," Castro nodded crisply. "Let's start with the schedule."

The rules of the game. When the court day would start, when it would end, when they would take lunch. Who would be testifying and when. How many prospective jurors they would question. How many alternate jurors they would seat in addition to the standard twelve, in case any of the jurors became unable to continue given the expected length of the trial. Every judge had their own personal preferences for those sorts of matters.

Raine had learned long ago not to have any preferences of his own. There would be plenty to fight over, but the person he was fighting was Stone, not Castro, and honestly, he really didn't care what time they adjourned at the end of the day, or whether they questioned fifty prospective jurors or a hundred. It was his job to be ready no matter how those questions were resolved. His job was to win no matter what the rules were.

Stone, on the other hand, felt the need to weigh in on every possible decision. She wanted to adjourn at 4:45, not 5:00 or 4:30. She wanted three alternate jurors, not two or four. She wanted this, not that or that.

In the end, Judge Castro listened to Stone's arguments then ruled the way she was always going to rule anyway. Perhaps

Stone was putting on a show for her clients. Raine didn't begrudge her that. They all had bills to pay. But she didn't get half of what she asked for. If her clients were paying attention, and they seemed like they were, they must have noticed their lawyer was already losing more than she was winning. Finch, on the other hand, watched his lawyer sit calmly and navigate the waves, rather than claim to be able to master them.

It took most of the first day to establish the rules with sufficient precision and clarity to proceed to the next step: selecting the referees. Fifty prospective jurors were brought into Castro's courtroom and the lawyers took turns asking them questions, in alternating twenty-minute sessions. Stone had asked for thirty. There were a lot of prospective jurors on the panel. There were a lot of parties and lawyers. And there were a lot of questions asked. In theory, the lawyers were only supposed to be trying to determine if there was anyone on the panel who, for whatever reason, wouldn't be able to follow the law as it applied to the case. Perhaps someone had personal experience with a similar situation or case. Perhaps someone had strong opinions about the justice system. Perhaps someone had nonrefundable tickets to Hawaii next week.

After the twenty-minute sessions of talking to the entire panel at once, there were always jurors who needed to be questioned in private, jurors who had a reason why they might not be fit for the jury but that reason was especially personal. All in all it took the entire first week to select the jurors who would hear the case. Twelve regular jurors, and four alternates. Not three. Castro swore the jurors in and then adjourned the trial for the weekend.

The following Monday morning arrived soon enough

and it was time for opening statements. The first two punches. Finally. And the plaintiff always went first.

"Ladies and gentlemen of the jury," Judge Castro announced when everyone was properly assembled in the courtroom, "please give your attention to Ms. Stone, who will deliver the opening statement on behalf of the plaintiffs."

24

"Thank you, Your Honor." Stone stood up from the plaintiff's counsel table and straightened her suit coat. They had solved the issue of too few chairs by having one parent from each family sit with her each day, alternating in a pattern designed to make sure the jury saw every possible permutation of the parents at the table. Stone squeezed behind Hailey's mother and Veronica's father and looked up to Judge Castro. "May it please the Court."

It was an old-fashioned thing to say before doing anything of import in a courtroom. Some lawyers thought it made them sound formal and professional. Others, like Raine, thought it made you sound pretentious and self-important. He hoped at least some of the jurors agreed.

Stone turned then to face the jurors and took up a spot directly in front of the jury box. She took a deep breath, offered a subdued smile, and began.

"They say the worst thing that can happen to a parent is the death of a child. But it's worse when the death was preventable. And it's even worse when the death was the result of someone else's negligence. In this case, we will show you that not one, but two wonderful young women died because of the negligence of the defendant," she pointed at him, "Duncan Finch."

The jurors all looked over at Finch, and by extension, Raine.

Raine had warned Finch about it—it was a standard ploy to point at the defendant during opening statement—and told him to look both remorseful and defiant. Remorseful that the women had lost their lives, but defiant in the face of the accusation that he was somehow responsible. Raine snuck a glance at his client to see how he was doing. He looked like he needed to go to the bathroom.

Stone continued. "Duncan Finch is the owner of The Finch Gallery, an upscale art gallery located right here in downtown Seattle, only a few blocks from the courthouse. He provides gallery space for art exhibitions. It's important to understand that getting your artwork in a gallery like The Finch Gallery is the dream of every artist. It's not just the thrill of seeing your work hanging on a gallery wall. It's the opportunities such exposure can provide to a young artist. Getting your work into a place like The Finch Gallery can literally be the difference between success or failure as an artist. Duncan Finch knew that. And he loved it."

Ah, the ad hominem *attack*, Raine noted. Well, like he told Sommers, every story needs a bad guy. Stone needed Finch to be craven and power hungry, rather than anxious and bad with money.

"You will hear," Stone continued, "about two particular art students who were the victims of Duncan Finch's need to be better than the artists whose fate he literally controlled. Their names were Hailey Parker and Veronica Kwon, and seated at my table right now are Hailey's mother and Veronica's father. Both the Parkers and the Kwons lost their daughters to the cruelty of Duncan Finch. Let me tell you first about Hailey Parker."

Stone was laying it on thick that Finch was an evil genius. Raine expected Hailey and Veronica were about to be sainted.

"Hailey was an artist. Her talent was obvious even from a very early age and her parents encouraged her to pursue her passion. By the time she finished high school, she had decided to try to become a full-time artist. She enrolled in the Cascadia Art School, again here in Seattle, just north of the Belltown neighborhood. It was a dream come true to be accepted into their program and she threw herself into her studies. It was very difficult, but very fulfilling. She had found her place. She had found her people."

Raine stifled an eye roll at the cliché. Jurors hated eye rolls.

"And then came an amazing opportunity, exactly the sort of opportunity she had hoped for when enrolling at Cascadia. The director of the school, Selina Thorne, had secured a special showing just for Cascadia students at the exclusive Finch Gallery. The gallery would feature the art of the school's students. Students like Hailey. She didn't know how Ms. Thorne had convinced a man like Duncan Finch to open his doors to artists still trying to break in, but she was thrilled by the opportunity. What she didn't know was that Duncan Finch would, callously and capriciously, destroy that opportunity, throwing into doubt her ability ever to succeed as the artist she knew she was."

Stone threw a rehearsed glare at Finch.

For his part, Finch looked hurt by the gesture. Raine supposed that was good.

"Duncan Finch had agreed to open his gallery to the students of Cascadia Art School," Stone continued. "He knew how important it was to them. But he wanted them to know how important *he* was to them, and to their hopes for any future success. So, he decided to exclude one student, not because their artwork wasn't up to standards, but just to remind them that he could. He chose one student to destroy. He chose Hailey Parker. And he succeeded in destroying her, far, far too literally."

"That's not what happened at all," Finch felt compelled to whisper in Raine's ear, despite Raine's direction not to talk to him when he was concentrating on the proceedings.

"I know," Raine whispered back, patting Finch on the arm in case any of the jurors were watching. "Now don't say another word. I need to listen."

"Hailey was excluded from the show," Stone went on, "but she attended the show anyway. Before leaving for the gallery, Hailey had concealed a small caliber handgun in her purse. She tried to support her friends, but it was all too much. Duncan Finch's arbitrary, capricious, and cruel actions were too much. Shortly before the night was to end, Hailey retreated to the women's room. She extracted that handgun from her purse. And then she shot herself in the heart. All because of what Duncan Finch had done to her."

Raine stole a glance at the jurors. It was poor form to stare at the jurors to gauge their reactions to everything, but he wanted to see if any of them were buying what Stone was selling. Unfortunately, most of them seemed to be. Raine could hardly blame them—they hadn't heard his side of the story yet—but it still created a barrier he was going to have to overcome in his own opening statement.

"Now," Stone took a beat, "let me tell you about Veronica Kwon."

Raine leaned forward slightly. He wondered how Stone was going to blame Veronica's death on Finch.

"Veronica was Hailey's best friend," Stone told the jurors. "She had her art hanging on the wall the night of the exhibition at The Finch Gallery. Duncan Finch didn't steal Veronica's future. He stole her best friend."

Ah, Raine realized.

"Veronica tried to carry on after her best friend was taken from her," Stone said, "and she might have managed to do so if Duncan Finch hadn't insisted on holding a second exhibition of Cascadia art students' work. The trauma of Hailey's suicide had barely subsided when Duncan Finch demanded an additional show of his power over students like Veronica, like Hailey. Veronica went to the exhibition. She put her artwork on the walls. She spent the evening in the gallery. But that was the same gallery where her best friend had been driven to suicide. Veronica was overcome by sadness at the loss of her friend, by shame at having returned for another exhibition despite what had happened to Hailey, and ultimately by an overwhelming feeling of helplessness in the face of men like Duncan Finch. She followed her best friend and committed suicide in The Finch Gallery, using a box cutter she found in a storage closet to slit her own throat."

Stone sighed and glanced around the courtroom, shaking her head slightly at the tragedy of it all, or something. She let her gaze linger accusingly on Finch, then returned it fully to the jurors. "Ladies and gentlemen, two wonderful, vibrant, talented young women are dead because of the capricious and cruel actions of the defendant. You are about to hear from the witnesses who will confirm everything I just told you. And when they are done and you've received all of the evidence in this case, I am going to stand before you again and ask you to find Duncan Finch and The Finch Gallery liable for the tragic deaths of Hailey Parker and Veronica Kwon. Thank you."

Stone returned to her seat and Judge Castro instructed the jurors, "Now, ladies and gentlemen, please give your attention to Mr. Raine, who will deliver the opening statement on behalf of the defendant."

The problem Raine faced was that he couldn't actually tell the jury what he expected to prove. Not yet. If he told them the real reason they were all there was that Stone's firm had a third client who wanted to buy Finch's gallery at a discount and they were using the tragedies of Hailey Parker and Veronica Kwon to drive down the price, he'd never succeed in extracting that evidence. It was a surprise and it needed to remain a surprise. But he had to say something. So, he decided to at least defend his client. And maybe throw out a clue of his real defense.

He stood up, buttoned his suit coat, and very decidedly did not say, 'May it please the Court.' It didn't matter if the Court was pleased. He wanted to please the jury. He walked directly to a very intentional spot directly in front of the jury box, close enough to spark the jurors' attention, but not so close as to come across as aggressive. He rooted himself to that spot and began.

"The Duncan Finch Ms. Stone described to you sure sounds like a terrible person. The kind of person you would feel okay holding liable for the deaths of two admittedly wonderful, talented young women. That's by design. You're supposed to hate him. It's easier to find against him if you hate him. But that man, the one Ms. Stone just told you about—he doesn't exist." Raine could point at his client too. "Duncan Finch isn't a monster. He's a lover of art, and of artists, and he absolutely, completely, and totally is not responsible for the deaths of either Hailey Parker or Veronica Kwon."

Raine paused to let that last sentence sink in. It was the bottom line of his case. He wanted the jurors to sit with it, even for just a moment.

"The problem with Ms. Stone's character assassination of Mr. Finch is that it doesn't quite add up. She told you he was the successful owner of an exclusive art gallery in downtown Seattle. But she also told you that he opened that exclusive art gallery to a group of young art students, students who might never again see their art hanging in a gallery." He put a thoughtful hand to his chin. "So, which is it? Is he a cruel gallery owner who wants to lord over lowly starving artists? Or is he a generous art lover who wanted to give some local young artists a taste of the success they were chasing, for no reason other than the goodness of his heart? I would submit to you that it has to be the latter, because the former makes no sense. The best way to keep those art students in their place is to never let them within a hundred yards of his successful and exclusive gallery. The man Ms. Stone described would never have arranged the exhibition in the first place, and that's something Ms. Stone is never going to be able to explain. The Finch Gallery only exists because of Duncan Finch's love and support of Seattle's artist community. I can tell you, if someone else were ever to buy that space, it would cease to be an art gallery."

Raine really wanted to turn around and gauge Stone's reaction to that last comment, but that would have been too much of a giveaway. He was just planting seeds. He'd water them during Stone's case-in-chief, then reap them when he put Caleb Marquardt on the stand in his own case.

"During the course of this trial, you're going to hear from a lot of witnesses who know Duncan Finch personally. Some have known him for years. And to a person, they are going to tell you that Duncan is a good man, a lover of the arts, and someone who would never treat someone the way Ms. Stone just described his alleged treatment of Hailey Parker. He was just trying to do a good deed, but as they say, no good deed goes unpunished. So here we all are. Two pairs of parents are hurting because they both lost daughters, but neither of those deaths was Duncan Finch's fault. This trial isn't about picking a winner and a loser between Duncan on the one hand and the Parkers and Kwons on the other. There has already been too much loss. This trial is about making sure no more loss is inflicted."

That was about all Raine wanted to say then. He would have a lot more to say in his closing argument.

"So, in conclusion," he said, "I ask you to keep an open mind. Open to the truth that Duncan is a good man. Open to the truth that sometimes bad things happen that can't be blamed on other people. And open to the truth that Duncan Finch is not liable for the deaths of either Hailey Parker or Veronica Kwon. Thank you."

The first two punches had been thrown, although Raine had pulled his a bit. Still, the fight was finally on. It was time to bring other people into it.

"Ms. Stone," Judge Castro looked down at her, "you may call your first witness."

25

As the plaintiffs' attorney, Stone had the burden of proof. That is, she had to prove what she alleged in her complaint—that Finch was liable for the deaths of Hailey Parker and Veronica Kwon. That meant she put her case on first, because if she failed to prove her allegations, then the case would simply be dismissed. Raine wouldn't have to call any witnesses of his own. Knowing that she was going to put on her case-in-chief first, Stone was able to structure it in advance. She could decide exactly which witnesses to call in what order and not worry about having to adjust to the other side's case the way Raine was going to have to do. She made the obvious decision on which witness to call first. And it was obvious because they were exactly the right witness to call first.

"Thank you, Your Honor." Stone stood to announce, "We call Susan Parker to the stand."

Hailey's mom.

Raine braced himself for the oncoming emotional onslaught.

Susan Parker stood up from her spot at the plaintiff's table and stepped forward to be sworn in by the judge. She was dressed simply in a black suit. She was, after all, in mourning.

Judge Castro raised her right hand and instructed Susan to do the same. "Do you swear or affirm that you will tell the truth, the whole truth, and nothing but the truth?"

"I do," Susan confirmed.

"Please be seated on the witness stand."

Susan followed the judge's instruction and in a moment was sitting in the witness stand, looking expectantly at the attorney she had hired to punish someone for what had happened to her daughter. Raine wondered how she was going to feel when she discovered she was being used as part of a real estate scam.

Stone took up a position in what was called 'the well,' the empty floor space between the lawyers' tables, the judge's bench, the witness stand, and the jury box. She stood close enough to her client to convey connection, but not too close. Too close was for cross-examination.

"Could you please state your name for the record?" Stone began the examination.

"Susan Marie Parker," came the response.

"Thank you for being here today, Ms. Parker."

It wasn't a question, but Raine was hardly going to object to a little humanity. He would be objecting soon enough to other things, he expected.

"Could you please tell the jury how you knew Hailey Parker?" Stone continued.

Susan turned to the men and women assembled to her right. "Hailey was my daughter."

There was a catch in her throat as she delivered the

answer, but she hadn't started crying quite yet. Raine supposed it was coming. He also supposed there was nothing he could do about it.

Stone then launched into a series of questions about Hailey's childhood. The idea was to humanize Hailey to the jury, make them realize she was a real person with real thoughts, feelings, and dreams. There were a lot of questions about Hailey's artistic interests. She started drawing at a very early age. She showed a knack for drawing horses. Her favorite gift on her birthdays was always the new art set. She designed her high school yearbook cover. Raine sat patiently through all of it, listening but not bothered. It wasn't until they got through Hailey's enrollment and potential participation in Finch's exhibition that Raine was ready to pounce.

"Did Hailey express any excitement about this exhibition at The Finch Gallery?" Stone asked.

"Oh yes," Susan answered. "Ever since she was a little girl, we had been taking her to art museums and art galleries. She would always say, "Momma, some day one of my paintings will be here,' and I knew she was right. It was finally happening and she was just so happy. I could hear that little girl in her voice when she told me about it."

"But then something happened, didn't it?" Stone asked. "Something that meant her dream of having her artwork hanging in a gallery wouldn't be happening after all?"

"Yes," Susan answered with a deep frown.

"What happened?"

"She called me crying," Susan recounted. "She was so upset, I couldn't even understand her at first. I told her I needed her to calm down enough to tell me what was going on and that's when she told me she wasn't going to get her art in the gallery after all."

"Did she tell you why?"

"Objection!" Raine popped to his feet. "Calls for hearsay."

Raine had been sitting quietly for so long at that point that most of the people in the courtroom had probably forgotten he was even there.

Judge Castro certainly looked surprised to hear from him, but she took a beat, then turned to Stone. "Response, counsel?"

"I'm asking if the witness knows why her daughter's artwork was not going to be displayed," Stone explained.

"And the only way she would know that is if her daughter told her what someone else told her daughter," Raine jumped in. "That's hearsay."

Judge Castro nodded slightly. "That does sound like hearsay, Ms. Stone. I'll sustain the objection. You may rephrase the question, if you wish."

Stone pursed her lips and exhaled audibly, her irritation not at all concealed. "Without telling me what she said, did Hailey explain to you why her artwork wasn't going to be displayed?"

"Yes, she did," Susan confirmed.

"And what did she say?" Stone tried.

But Raine repeated his objection. "That's still hearsay, Your Honor. If anything, counsel just made it even more clear that this witness would just be repeating back what someone else told her."

Raine was willing to die on this particular hill. Stone had to deliver on her promises in opening statement, and one of those promises was that Finch was the one who rejected Hailey Parker's art, and that he did so maliciously. Finch was going to deny that, and Thorne would at least dispute that there wasn't any malice. No one else had first-hand knowledge of the decision-making process, so Raine needed to make sure Stone didn't slip in her claims through some third-party witness who wasn't involved in the decision.

"I will sustain the objection," Castro repeated. "This witness will not be allowed to testify as to why a certain decision were made if she only learned about it secondhand. Ask a different question."

Stone was even more upset than after Raine's first objection was sustained. She flipped impatiently through her notes. "Fine, Your Honor," she huffed. "Let's move ahead to the night of the exhibition. The night of Hailey's death."

Raine sat down again. He would be vigilant about limiting any testimony about why Hailey's artwork was rejected, but he was going to do his best to blend away while Hailey's mom talked about her daughter's death.

That was when the tears started. She recounted being at home that evening, feeling bad for her daughter's exclusion from the show, but unsure how to make it all better for her little girl. And then she got a call from the police. Her daughter was dead, they said. Suicide. And she knew why. Oh, she knew why.

Stone mopped up with a series of questions about the funeral and the unbearable burden of burying your own child, then finished with her obviously preplanned final question.

"Do you still miss Hailey, Ms. Parker?"

"Every day." Susan Parker stifled a sob. "Every day."

"Thank you, Ms. Parker." Stone looked up to the judge. "No further questions, Your Honor." She returned to her seat next to Philip Kwon.

Judge Castro cast her eye down on the defense table. "Cross-examination, Mr. Raine?"

Raine stood up. "No questions, Your Honor."

You don't cross-examine the mom.

There was no upside to questioning a grieving mother. If Raine was aggressive with her, the jury would hate him. If he wasn't aggressive, it would just be an opportunity for her to repeat everything she had already said on direct examination. On the other hand, he could look like a nice guy for not going after Hailey's mom, and maybe some of that goodwill would rub off on Finch.

In any event, Susan Parker was done on the witness stand. The judge excused her back to her seat next to her attorney.

"You may call your next witness," Judge Castro instructed.

Stone stood again. The plaintiffs would call Philip Kwon to the stand.

Raine leaned back in his chair. *Here we go again.*

———

PHILIP KWON PROVIDED ESSENTIALLY the same testimony about his daughter as Susan Parker had about hers. A similar back story about drawing horses and a bucket of markers and colored pencils.

When Stone tried to elicit the reasons for Hailey Parker's exclusion from the show, Raine again objected to it as hearsay and Judge Castro again sustained the objection. Philip Kwon could testify about his observations and experiences regarding his own daughter, but he could not tell the jury what Veronica had told him that Hailey told her that

Thorne told her about why her artwork wouldn't be at the exhibition.

Raine felt like the first two witnesses were a draw. Stone humanized her clients, but Raine blocked her from demonizing his.

Those two witnesses had taken the entire first day. Castro adjourned the case and they came back the next morning for more witnesses. It was time to move on from the families.

Upon invitation from the judge, Stone stood up and announced, "The plaintiffs call Selina Thorne to the stand."

26

Raine's heart raced a bit at the sound of Selina Thorne's name. He wasn't a teenager anymore, but he wasn't dead yet either. He was also a professional. He would enjoy watching her testify on the stand, but no one would know.

Thorne entered the courtroom from the hallway, where witnesses had to wait while other witnesses testified, and made her way to the front of the courtroom to be sworn in. She wore a long, flowy ensemble that looked like it might have aspects of a suit mixed into what was otherwise mostly a dress.

Judge Castro raised her right hand and asked Thorne whether she swore or affirmed that she would tell the truth, the whole truth, and nothing but the truth.

"I do," Thorned answered.

She floated onto the witness stand and Stone began her questioning.

It was the same set of introductory questions. It was always the same, for every witness.

Name? "Selina Thorne."

Occupation? "I'm the Director of the Cascadia Art School."

How did you know Hailey Parker and/or Veronica Kwon? "They were my students."

Stone spent a little time on the history of the school. Thorne had spent time as a starving artist, but started teaching art lessons on the side to be able to afford things like food. Eventually she discovered she was at least as good a teacher as an artist. Her one-time lessons here and there turned into tutoring gigs. The tutoring gigs led to teaching an adult education class at a community college. That job led to contacts throughout the art education world. She taught for a few different schools for a few different years until eventually she ventured out on her own and founded Cascadia Art School, the culmination of her years of hard work and dedication as an artist and educator.

Raine was enraptured. There was so much he wanted to discover about Selina Thorne. But not until after the trial.

"I'd like to turn your attention now to an event proposed to be held at The Finch Gallery here in Seattle," Stone said. "Were you involved in the planning of that event?"

"I was the one who proposed the event," Thorne answered.

"Did you approach Mr. Finch directly with the idea?"

"Yes."

"How did you know Mr. Finch?" Stone asked.

"I knew him both professionally and personally," Thorne explained. "Professionally, we traveled in a lot of the same circles. Swam in the same ponds, you might say, and there aren't that many ponds for artists. You tend to see the same people over and over. Eventually I came to think of him not only as a colleague, but a friend. When I got the idea of doing an actual gallery showing for our students, I thought his space would be perfect."

"How did Mr. Finch react to your proposal?" Stone asked.

Thorne considered for a moment before answering. "I would say he was intrigued by it. He was concerned about giving up time and space that might otherwise generate him income, so we had to work through that. I suggested we put it on on a Tuesday night, when he wouldn't have had much foot traffic anyway, and I also proposed turning it into a fundraiser, with him receiving a share for his fee."

"So, he did charge you for the use of his gallery?" Stone asked.

"Yes," Thorne confirmed.

"He didn't do it out of the kindness of his heart?"

Thorne shrugged. "I can't say that wasn't part of it as well, but he didn't do it for free."

Raine frowned slightly. Everyone needed to get paid, but everyone was also quick to judge others for doing so.

"I'd like to talk now about how artwork was selected for the show," Stone said. She turned to Raine. "Unless there's an objection," she invited.

It was a smart play, Raine admired. Get his hearsay challenges out of the way in advance. It would prevent interruptions to the flow of her examination, and if the judge was going to sustain his objections, calling them out in advance prevented her from looking foolish later.

He stood up. "We will not be objecting to this witness recounting any conversations she had with Mr. Finch regarding the selection of artwork for the exhibit," Raine advised the Court. "Those statements would have been heard firsthand by this witness, they would have a non-hearsay use as oral confirmation of agreement, and they would be admissible as statements of a party opponent in any event."

Raine's response wasn't so much for the judge as for everyone else in the courtroom. He could have just told the judge, 'No objection,' but he wanted the jurors and Stone to know he was a smart and knowledgeable advocate. He didn't mind Thorne seeing it too.

Judge Castro nodded at Raine's recitation. "Thank you, Mr. Raine. You may proceed, Ms. Stone."

"Please explain to the jury the process that was employed to select artwork for the exhibition," Stone instructed, "and who made those decisions."

Raine was counting on Thorne to soft pedal it to the jury. She had just called Finch a friend after all. He didn't need her to say the decision was hers. He just needed her to say it was fair. Hailey's work just wasn't ready yet. That's what she had told him the night of the gala. She just needed to say it one more time.

"It had been my intent," Thorne turned and delivered her answer directly to the jurors, "that every single one of my students get the opportunity to see their artwork displayed in the gallery. I thought Mr. Finch was in agreement with that, but as the date for the exhibition approached, he started to voice concerns over available space. He didn't think it was a good look for his gallery to have paintings practically touching each other, or leaned against the walls in the hallway. He insisted that we pare down the number of works to be displayed. I wasn't comfortable with that, but it was too late to cancel, so I did the best I could."

"And what was the best you could do?" Stone followed up. "Were you able to get every student's art into the show?"

Thorne frowned. "No, I wasn't."

"Whose artwork was not included in the show?"

"Hailey Parker's," Thorne confirmed what everyone already knew.

"Anyone else?"

"No," Thorne answered. "Just Hailey."

"And do you know why Mr. Finch selected Hailey Parker for exclusion from the show?"

Raine had asked Thorne the same question the first night they met, right there in the gallery. Hailey's work wasn't quite good enough. *Just say that again.*

Thorne again turned to the jury and told them something completely different. "As I recall, Mr. Finch insisted that one student be excluded," she testified. "I'm not sure why or how he came to select Hailey. It appeared to be random. But I was left with the choice of trying to explain to one student why her artwork wouldn't be on the gallery walls, or backing out of the event and having to explain that to all of my students." She dropped her head and sighed. "I chose wrong."

Raine's jaw fell open. Finch was beside himself.

"That's not true," Finch whisper-yelled at him. "That's not what happened at all. She told me Hailey's work wasn't good enough and I went along with that."

"I know, I know," Raine tried to calm his client down. "And you'll get your chance to tell the jury all that." But the damage had already been done.

"No further questions," Stone announced.

"Any cross-examination, Mr. Raine?" Judge Castro asked.

Raine stood up. "Yes, Your Honor." There was no way he

could leave that testimony unchallenged. But it was difficult to challenge without knowing why she had said it.

He stepped out from behind his counsel table and approached the witness stand. He got one step too close, the perfect position for cross-examination. "You just testified that it was Mr. Finch who decided to exclude Hailey Parker's work from the show at his gallery; is that correct?"

Thorne nodded. "Yes, I did just say that."

"But isn't it true that you told me the night of the exhibition that Hailey's work wasn't quite up to standards for the show?"

"The night of the exhibition?" Thorne frowned. "I may have said that, but if I did, I believe I was trying to spare Hailey the details of what had really happened."

Raine cocked his head. "You thought it would be less hurtful to know that she had been excluded at random rather than because she wasn't good enough?"

"That may sound strange," Thorne allowed, "but in my experience, there are things you can control and then there are things that are inflicted on you by others. As long as you believe things are within your control, you will work hard to improve and succeed. It's when you get old and cynical and realize that things happen to you for no reason—that's when you start to give up. I didn't want Hailey to have to learn that lesson so young."

Raine rubbed a hand over his chin. Not only had she told the jury exactly what Stone wanted them to hear, she had not denied her earlier contradictory statement. Instead, she acknowledged it and then spun it to inflict even more damage on Finch. Was she really that afraid of being sued by the Parkers too? Finch was going to lose his gallery. Thorne must have been afraid she might lose her school.

Raine thought Thorne and Finch were friends. He wasn't sure he wanted to know what she might do to an enemy. But he was sure that he didn't want the jury to hear any more from her.

"No further questions, Your Honor," Raine practically conceded.

"Any redirect examination, Ms. Stone?" Judge Castro asked.

Stone stood up. "No, Your Honor."

Castro nodded. "May this witness be excused, or shall she remain subject to recall?"

An excused witness was officially finished with the case and could sit through the testimony of other witnesses, if they so chose. A witness who was subject to recall might have to testify again and therefore was still barred from the courtroom. Raine had intended to call Thorne again in his case-in-chief, after Stone rested her case. Now, he wasn't so sure. But even in his stunned state, he knew to keep his options open.

"We would ask that this witness be subject to recall," he told the judge.

"Very well," Judge Castro replied. She advised Thorne she was free to go that day, but that she might be asked to return to testify again later in the trial, so to please continue to remain outside the courtroom during any proceedings.

Thorne agreed and exited the courtroom. She didn't look at Raine as she passed, but that was fine with Raine. He didn't want to look at her either.

27

The remainder of Stone's witnesses took over a week to present, but none of them did more damage than Thorne had. It was a parade of other family members, other art students, and others involved in the case, one way or another. Raine cross-examined here and there, as seemed appropriate, but he was eager for Stone to finish putting on her witnesses so he could put on his.

As things stood, the jury had heard that it was definitely Finch who had excluded Hailey Parker's artwork, and for no apparent reason other than to demonstrate his control of the exhibition. That was one of two major pieces of the puzzle. The other was that Hailey Parker committed suicide. To establish that, Stone first called Detective Crenshaw to the stand to describe the crime scenes, then finished her case-in-chief with the medical examiner who had conducted the autopsies on both Hailey Parker and Veronica Kwon.

Raine's initial plan to attack the conclusion of suicide evaporated when he discovered Veronica Kwon's body in that storage closet. He might have been able to convince the jurors that maybe, just maybe, one of the dead women had been murdered by an unknown assailant, but he would lose all credibility if he suggested that for both deaths.

Dr. Emily Sanchez turned to the jury and delivered the last answer of her lengthy and at times overly technical testimony. "In both cases, I concluded that the manner of death was suicide."

That was also the final piece of Stone's case-in-chief. Dr. Sanchez was excused and Stone stood to declare, "We rest our case."

What followed was called 'halftime' by the lawyers, although it usually occurred well past the fifty percent mark of the trial. Plaintiffs had the burden of proof, so they went first and called a lot of witnesses. Defendants poked holes in the plaintiff's case. That required fewer witnesses and less time. Stone had taken almost two weeks to present all of her evidence. Raine would be lucky to take up two days.

Customarily, the Court would adjourn the case for the remainder of the day, allowing both sides time to prepare before the defendant launched their own case-in-chief the next morning. A defense attorney could waive that presumptive procedure and ask to go immediately into their case-in-chief, but most attorneys welcomed the opportunity to digest what had, and had not, been established by the plaintiff before resting their case, and make sure all of the defense ducks were in a row for an orderly presentation. Raine was certainly in that camp. Especially because he wanted to talk to Sommers before he did anything else.

Judge Castro adjourned the case until the next morning, and Raine and Finch walked back to his office to meet with Sommers. A light drizzle had moved in since the mostly sunny morning. Nothing too wet, but it lowered the air temperature noticeably. Raine put up the collar on his suit coat and quickened his gait. Finch struggled to keep up.

When they got to Raine's office, his hair was damp, his face was cold, and his client was out of breath. Sommers, warm and dry, was inside waiting for them.

"You walked?" She was incredulous. "You know there are cars, right? Or at least umbrellas."

"The only people who use umbrellas in Seattle are tourists," Raine replied. He pulled off his damp coat and shook the rain off it. "I'm fine. We're fine. What have you got for us?"

Sommers smiled and extracted a large envelope from her bag. "Only exactly what you wanted me to get. And what you'll need to win the case."

"Can we sit down somewhere?" Finch asked. "I'm exhausted from that run from the courthouse."

"We walked," Raine said.

"You walked," Finch replied. "I had to run to keep up."

Raine decided to take the complaint as a compliment. Maybe he wasn't as out of shape as he felt sometimes. "Sure," he answered Finch's request. "Let's go to the conference room. We'll have room to spread out whatever Rebecca has managed to secure for us."

His conference room didn't have a view of Elliott Bay or the Olympic Mountains, but it had a large table, and chairs. Finch dropped himself into a chair. Sommers dropped the contents of the envelope onto the table.

"It took some doing," she said, "but I finally managed to connect Caleb to the case."

"Caleb?" Finch asked. "Caleb Marquardt? What does he have to do with this?"

"Maybe everything," Raine answered. "He wants to buy the gallery out from under you."

"At a discount," Sommers added.

"And his lawyer is Amanda Stone," Raine finished.

Finch was speechless.

Raine was considerably less so. "What did you find?" he asked.

"I had to call in a lot of markers," Sommers began. "I stretched the limits of a few of my relationships. But I got what we needed. I got Caleb's signature on documents related to each of the three prior transactions."

"Really?" Raine didn't try to hide his excitement. "What kind of documents?"

"Not the actual purchase-and-sale agreements," Sommers admitted. "Those were all signed in the name of the corporation. But there's always some small detail behind the scene. Caleb signed off on the pre-purchase building inspections. That's the kind of form that never gets filed with any public entity, but which any good realtor will hold on to, just in case there are problems down the road. And if that particular realtor or realtors owed me a favor for, say, I don't know, offering them a listing that ended up in the biggest sale of their career, that person might have been willing to send a copy of some perfunctory inspection report that was just sitting in a file somewhere anyway."

"I-I don't think I understand," Finch stammered.

"You tell him, Rebecca," Raine suggested, "while I inspect the documents you brought me."

So, Sommers explained it all. Marquardt just needed to buy Finch's building and he could sell the entire block at an astronomical mark-up. And he was using the suicides of Hailey Parker and Veronica Kwon to drive down the price on the gallery. For all they knew, Caleb and his corporate lawyer Churchill, Walmer, and Pickwick had met with Amanda Stone to hatch a plan to recruit first the Parkers and then the Kwons as clients in order to sue Finch. It was complex and secretive, but Rebecca had cracked it, and Raine had the proof.

"So, wait." Finch was becoming increasingly distressed. "You're saying Caleb Marquardt owns the three other buildings on my block?"

"Yes, exactly," Raine answered.

"He never told us that," Finch complained. "Why wouldn't he tell us that? We could have been partners."

"Partners share things," Sommers explained. "I thought Caleb was a friend, but really, he's a psychopath."

"He's a motive," Raine said. "The motive for suing you. It's not because you're in any way responsible for the deaths of those two young women. It's just to lower the sales price."

Raine smiled at the documents Sommers had procured for him. "Oh, I'm going to have fun tomorrow."

28

W hen the trial first began, Raine expected to call three witnesses: Selina Thorne, Caleb Marquardt, and Duncan Finch. Raine had three goals. Refute the alleged reason for the suicides, give the jury the real reason for the lawsuits, and unequivocally profess his client's innocence.

Thorne was supposed to accomplish the first goal by telling the jury that it was at least partially her decision to exclude Hailey Parker from the showing. Marquardt would accomplish the second goal, albeit without prior knowledge, by allowing Raine to confront him about his purchases of the other buildings on the block, his penchant for buying properties under market value, and the fact that the attorneys who helped him do that were the same ones suing Finch. And the last goal would be met when Finch took the stand, after all of that other information had been revealed, to look the jurors in the eye and tell them unequivocally that he was innocent.

But that plan went sideways as soon as Thorne told the

jury that the decision to exclude Hailey's work was Finch's alone. Raine couldn't call Thorne back to the stand just to repeat the damaging testimony she previously gave. That meant he had to begin with Marquardt. But he didn't want either Thorne or Marquardt to know his plans had changed, lest either or both of them realized why. So, Raine made every effort to appear as if he hadn't changed strategies. He told both Thorne and Marquardt to come to court and be ready to testify. They would simply assume Thorne would testify after Marquardt, until Raine forced Marquardt to admit his connection to Stone's law firm and his personal financial interest in the outcome of the case.

Sommers had missed all but a few glimpses of the trial up until then, but she wasn't about to miss what promised to be the most important testimony in the case. Raine met her in the lobby of the courthouse and they made their way together to Judge Castro's courtroom. As they approached, they saw Thorne and Marquardt both already waiting outside the courtroom doors. Raine frowned as he noticed they were doing that thing again where Marquardt was standing too close to Thorne and she couldn't seem to decide what to do about it. They were engaged in a whispered and spirited debate about something they both seemed to find very important.

"Look," Marquardt was saying, "we're almost through this. Just stay the course and all of this will be behind us soon enough."

Thorne nodded. "I know. I just want to be finished with this entire, dreadful business."

"Me too, Selina," Marquardt consoled her.

"That makes three of us," Raine spoke up and made his presence known. "Four if you count Rebecca."

Thorne and Marquardt both jumped at the sound of his voice.

"We were just—" Thorne started.

"This whole thing—" Marquardt struggled to add.

"It's just so—" Thorne tried again.

"I understand," Raine assured them. "Believe me, I really do understand. And I promise, when we're done here today, the jury will know the truth."

"Well, that's probably good," Thorne allowed.

"Of course it's good," Marquardt boomed with a suddenly confident grin. "The truth is always good."

Raine had to smile at that. "I'm glad you feel that way, Caleb. You'll be my first witness. You can both have a seat out here in the hallway. I'll come and get you when it's your time."

———

RAINE AND SOMMERS entered the courtroom together, but then Sommers took a seat in the gallery while Raine made his way to the defense table. It had been a long time since he and Finch stopped trying to coordinate their arrivals. It was a sort of extra service he provided at the beginning of the trial, when Finch was unsure how to get to the courtroom or where to sit once he arrived. But after weeks in trial, Finch was already seated in his usual seat when Raine walked up to the table to unpack his briefcase and wish his client a good morning.

Stone was also already there. They too had adjusted their interactions. The first days, they would greet each other each day, even if coldly. By the second week they might offer a grunt or maybe a nod. That morning, they ignored each other completely. They could talk to each other when the judge came out, which happened in short order. Early arrivals had also given way to just-in-time arrivals.

"All rise!" the bailiff called the courtroom to order when Judge Castro entered.

"Please be seated," she bade the lawyers and parties in her courtroom as she had done every day since the trial began. But she was ready to get right to business too. "Are your witnesses here, Mr. Raine? I'd like to get started as soon as we can this morning."

Raine stood to answer the judge. "Yes, Your Honor. Our first witness is waiting in the hallway right now."

"Good," Castro commented. "How many witnesses do you think we can get through today?"

Raine wasn't sure how to answer. Marquardt's testimony might not take all that long—although it might, depending on how much he resisted Raine's questioning. It was the fallout that was likely to take the most time. When Raine accused Amanda Stone and Churchill, Walmer, and Pickwick of manufacturing a wrongful death lawsuit to benefit another client's real estate investments, well, the courtroom was going to explode. He was kind of looking forward to it.

"Hard to say, Your Honor," Raine answered. "I guess we should just get started and see how things go."

It wasn't a terribly original suggestion, but everyone knew that was how it would proceed. That was trial work. Anything could happen.

"Bring out the jury!" Judge Castro instructed her bailiff.

A few minutes later, everyone was once again assembled for another day of the same trial.

"Mr. Raine," Judge Castro inquired formally, "does the defendant wish to call any witnesses?"

Raine stood and answered just as formally. "Yes, Your Honor. The defendant calls Caleb Marquardt to the stand."

He nodded to Sommers, who went to fetch Marquardt from the hallway.

He entered, tall and impeccably dressed, looking almost more calm and confident than he should have under the circumstances. But then again, he didn't know all of the circumstances. He thought he was going to testify about sponsoring a memorial scholarship fund. He didn't know Raine had other plans.

Judge Castro swore Marquardt in and he took his place on the witness stand.

Raine took up his position in the well, and began his examination. "Could you please state your name for the record?"

Raine had more than just a structure for his examination of Marquardt. They would, of course, start with the usual name, rank, and serial number. Caleb Nathaniel Marquardt. Investor, entrepreneur, patron of the arts. Acquaintances with the defendant, but he wouldn't call them friends exactly.

Normally, a direct examination would be structured for the benefit of the jury. It would be designed to present the most important information, in a logical and progressive manner. The witness was a vessel of the knowledge the lawyer wanted the jury to absorb. It was all about the jurors.

And while that was still an important part of Raine's plans for Marquardt's testimony, there was a predicate consideration, which was getting Marquardt to say that vital information in the first place. He wasn't going to just admit to wanting Finch to be sued so he could buy his gallery out from under him, with the help of the opposing law firm.

There was a reason he had gone to such efforts to conceal his involvement in such enterprises. He wasn't just going to confess because Raine asked him a question about it. Raine needed to soften him up first. Flatter him. Distract him. Overwhelm him. And then, when he was having trouble thinking straight because things were going too fast in too many directions, Raine could get him first to deny the real estate transactions, then hit him with the receipts, literally. Not only would the jury learn that Marquardt had a reason to want the Parkers and Kwons to sue Finch, they would experience exactly the sort of duplicity Raine would be accusing him of.

It was going to take a while.

After eliciting Marquardt's curriculum vitae and his relationship with Finch, Raine spent time flattering him. Or allowing him to flatter himself. Raine served him questions that allowed Marquardt to brag about his philanthropic proclivities and especially his support of the fine arts. He had been an early supporter of the first gala, and he was the official sponsor of the second gala, his name prominently displayed in the main hall for all the Seattle art world to see.

Having pumped him up, Raine turned next to lowering his defenses. Or numbing them rather. He would show Marquardt photos of the two dead women, sprawled in pools of their own blood. If Marquardt had any conscience at all, those photographs had a chance to reach it. And then, when his emotions were stirred up, Raine would finally pounce on the real estate transaction he and Stone's firm were trying to hide.

Raine prepared the documents he would need, so that he could hand them to Marquardt rapid-fire, to overcome his ability to think before speaking. There were five exhibits:

three signed inspection reports for each of the purchases of
the other buildings on the block, a police photograph of
Hailey Parker's body on the floor of the bathroom, and one
of his own photographs of Veronica Kwon on the floor of the
storage room.

Finch watched him extract the exhibits from his case file
and set them up carefully on the table they shared. Raine
didn't think much of it—if nothing else, Finch's interest
would show the jury he was still engaged in his defense—
but then Finch tapped on the photo of Veronica Kwon dead
on the floor of his storage room.

"This is wrong," Finch said in something louder than a
whisper. "This is all wrong."

"Sorry, Duncan," Raine replied in a quieter voice. "I
know these kind of photos can be pretty upsetting if you're
not used to them, but I have a job to do."

"No, that's not what I meant," Finch said. "I mean they're
wrong. The things on the shelves—they're in all the wrong
places."

Raine looked at the photograph again. "What are you
talking about?"

"Are you ready to continue your examination, Mr.
Raine?" Judge Castro prompted. Everyone was waiting
on him.

"Uh, just a moment, Your Honor," he answered. "I'm just
organizing some exhibits for my next area of inquiry. He
noticed Marquardt craning his neck slightly to try to see
what was on Raine's table.

"What are you talking about?" Raine repeated, definitely
in a whisper. "And keep your voice down."

Finch pointed at the photograph. "I'm talking about the
shelves," he whispered. "Nothing is where it's supposed to

be. I may not be the biggest man, or the strongest, or even the smartest, but I'm probably the tidiest. You don't run an art gallery if you don't have a flair for how things look. Those shelves are an absolute disaster. The paper products are mixed in with the canned goods with the cleaning supplies. You can't store canned peaches next to ammonia."

Raine picked up the photograph and examined it as if for the first time. There were no items on the floor; everything was shelved. But Finch was right. The items themselves were completely mixed up and out of order.

"And the shelves aren't even lined up properly," Finch gestured at the photograph, the volume of his voice increasing again. "Do you see that? That shelving unit in the middle is at least an inch farther forward than the one next to it. It's like someone pulled everything off the shelves, then put everything back with the lights off. My God, what even happened in there?"

Raine knew exactly what had happened in there. *Signs of a struggle.*

He hadn't planned for that in the structure of his direct examination. He was going to have to improvise. He was going to need to have a witness, any witness, testify that the photograph of Veronica Kwon looked like there had been a struggle.

He could have Finch say it, but he kind of liked the idea of having more than one witness reach the same conclusion. Raine had wanted the bloody photographs to stun Marquardt just before asking him his plan to steal Finch's gallery. But if he was going to show him the photos anyway, why not have him tell the jury a little about what was in them, and what conclusions might be drawn from them.

Raine picked up the photograph of Hailey Parker and

handed it to him. "Do you recognize what's depicted in this photograph, Mr. Marquardt?"

Marquardt frowned at the image. "It's a photo of Hailey Parker on the floor of the ladies' bathroom at Mr. Finch's gallery."

"How do you know that?"

"Because I was there that night," Marquardt answered. "I saw this scene with my own eyes."

"Do you know how she died?" Raine asked.

"Suicide," Marquardt answered firmly.

"I meant more specifically," Raine clarified. "How did she die?"

"Oh." Marquardt nodded. "She shot herself in the heart with a small-caliber handgun. A twenty-two, I think."

"And the image in that photograph," Raine pointed at the image, "does that appear to be consistent with her shooting herself in the chest?"

Marquardt shrugged. "Yes. She killed herself. I feel comfortable saying that."

Raine noted that response. Even the medical examiner wouldn't say with complete certainty that Hailey Parker's death was suicide and not murder.

"Very sad, isn't it?" Raine followed up.

"Oh, yes," Marquardt was quick to agree. "Definitely very sad."

Raine next fetched the photograph of Veronica Kwon and handed it to Marquardt. "Can you tell us what this is a photograph of?"

Marquardt examined the photograph. "It appears to be a photograph of the other woman who committed suicide at Mr. Finch's gallery."

"Do you feel confident saying that, Mr. Marquardt?"

Raine challenged him. "Do you feel confident saying Ms. Kwon committed suicide?"

"Uh, I mean, that's what the police said, isn't it?" Marquardt answered.

"The police said there were no signs of a struggle," Raine told him, "but perhaps you overheard Mr. Finch tell me just now that the entire room looks like there had been a significant struggle and then someone cleaned up the signs of it. Would you agree with that assessment?"

Marquardt looked at the photo, then lowered it again. "I guess. I don't know."

"Why do you know Hailey Parker's death was a suicide, but you don't know that Veronica Kwon's was?" Raine pressed. "What do you think the police will do if they agree with Mr. Finch's assessment? Do you think they'll go back and process the scene more thoroughly? Do you think they might decide it wasn't suicide?"

"I-I have no idea," Marquardt stammered. He looked nervously around the courtroom.

"Do you think they might catch the killer?" Raine asked. Because that would definitely get Finch off the hook, at least for the Kwon death.

"I'm not sure," Marquardt answered.

"Probably though," Raine suggested. "Don't you think?"

Marquardt didn't answer the question. That was fine with Raine; it was time to get to the pay-off. Marquardt seemed sufficiently shaken. More than Raine had expected actually. The jury needed to hear about his relationship with Churchill, Walmer, and Pickwick and how it was entangled in the case against Finch.

"Let me ask you a question, Mr. Marquardt," Raine

began. "How much experience do you have in commercial real—"

"It was me," Marquardt interjected.

Raine took a moment to assess what he heard, and if it could really mean what it appeared to mean. "I'm sorry?"

"It was me," Marquardt repeated. "I did it. I'm the one responsible for those women's deaths."

A murmur would have rippled through the courtroom except that everyone was stunned to absolute silence.

"You?" Raine broke the silence. "You're responsible? How?"

Stone stood to object, then withered under the gaze of Judge Castro. There was no way she was going to let anyone interfere in what was unfolding in her courtroom.

"Um, the first woman," Marquardt explained. "Hailey. She was upset that she didn't get her work in the show. She had been carrying that gun around because she was thinking about killing herself. I found out and told her I thought she should. It would be the ultimate performance art."

Raine just stared at Marquardt for several seconds. He was a psychopath. "What about Veronica Kwon?"

"Yeah, well, see, she found out about it," Marquardt said. "About what I did. She said she was going to tell the police. I couldn't let that happen. So I killed her."

"With a box cutter you found in the storage room?" Raine endeavored.

"Yes, exactly," Marquardt agreed. "That's what happened. A crime of passion using a weapon of convenience."

Raine took a few moments before he said anything further. Technically they were still in the middle of his direct examination, but for all intents and purposes the trial was over. Finch couldn't be found liable for deaths someone else confessed to causing. The only sounds in the courtroom were a mother's crying and Judge Castro telling her bailiff to call the marshals.

Finally he shook his head at Marquardt. "You're going to prison for the rest of your life. Do you understand that?"

Marquardt sighed. "Yes. I understand that completely."

29

The marshals arrested Marquardt where he sat on the witness stand. Judge Castro granted Raine's motion to dismiss the lawsuit. The jurors were released from the case. Stone stormed out of the courtroom without a word. Finch hugged Raine. And Sommers walked up to him and gave him the firmest congratulatory handshake he'd ever received.

"That was amazing!" she effused. "Did you have that planned all along? And you didn't tell anyone? Not even me? No wonder you wanted me here today, to witness your glorious victory."

Raine was as surprised as anyone that the case had suddenly collapsed out from under Amanda Stone. But he wasn't about to complain. And he was okay with people thinking he'd planned it all along. Sometimes luck was better than planning.

Stone didn't seem bothered by the turn of events. Marquardt had way more money than Finch, and he'd just confessed. He had literally said, "I'm the one responsible for those women's deaths." Stone would have to refile a new lawsuit, but there was no way she could lose. All in all, her job had just gotten easier.

"We should celebrate," Sommers said. "Dinner and drinks. The Rainier Bay Club. Everything goes on my tab."

"The Rainier Bay Club?" Raine confirmed. "Are you sure?"

"I'm sure," Sommers answered. "You've earned it."

"You sure have," Finch put in. "You saved my gallery. You saved everything. I don't know how to thank you."

Raine did, but he didn't want to talk fees just then. Now that he'd won the case, Finch would be able to generate the income he'd need to pay off his bill with Raine. It was a win for him too.

THE VIEWS from Sommers's usual table at the Rainier Bay Club were almost as amazing as the food. It was just Raine and Sommers. Finch decided to go back to his gallery and sit in the middle of it all night, so grateful was he not to have lost it.

"I still can't believe you got Caleb to just confess like that," Sommers said. "That was amazing to watch. I don't know how you did it."

Raine wasn't quite sure either. There was something in the back of his mind that was cutting against the celebration he was trying to enjoy.

Enough time had passed since the euphoria of the dismissal. He could be honest with his partner. He needed to be honest with her. "That wasn't where I was going with my questioning. I just wanted to mess with his head a little. Get him off balance before I hit him with those inspection receipts your contacts gave you. And then he confessed."

"Right after you told him the police were going to catch him anyway," Sommers recounted.

"I didn't say they were going to catch him specifically," Raine recalled. "I said they were going to catch the killer."

"Which was him, it turned out," Sommers pointed out.

Raine frowned. He finally realized what had been bothering him since the marshals stormed into the courtroom and snatched Marquardt off the witness stand.

"Did you see him at the second gallery show?" he asked. "I know he was the sponsor of the scholarship fund or whatever, but did you ever actually see him that night?"

Sommers thought for a few moments. "Actually, no, I don't think I did."

"And he testified that his sponsorship banner was prominently displayed in the main gallery," Raine recalled, "but I hid it by the coat check."

"Oh shit," Sommers realized.

"He wasn't there that night," Raine said. "He didn't kill Veronica Kwon."

But now they knew who did.

30

The outer doors weren't even locked. Raine and Sommers entered the building and made their way down the hall for their third visit to the office.

"You didn't even notice I'd left," Selina Thorne said when they walked into her office. "Caleb was dragged off in handcuffs, the judge dismissed the case, and you didn't even come out to the hallway to tell me."

Raine felt the urge to apologize. He fought it off.

"That's how I knew you knew," Thorne said. "If you had really believed him, you would have told me what he did. But you didn't. You took your victory while you could. I don't blame you. Caleb is chivalrous, in his own way, but he's not smart enough to pull it off. He thinks he loves me. That's why he did it. But he's not strong enough to see it all the way through."

"His lawyer will convince him to tell the truth."

Thorne laughed darkly. "Those damn lawyers," she said.

"So, why?" Raine asked. "Was Hailey's suicide really supposed to be performance art?"

"Is that what he said?" Thorne laughed again. "Oh, good for him. That really is excellent. But I'm afraid it's more complicated than that."

Thorne took a careful look at her guests, then went ahead and dropped into a chair. "Do you have any idea what it's like to be the teacher when all you ever wanted to be was the doer? To spend day after day, year after year helping others chase a dream you were forced to give up so long ago it seems like another lifetime?"

Raine knew they weren't actually supposed to answer any of those questions. Or the one coming next.

"Did you know your skills atrophy if you don't use them? Some people think painting would be like riding a bike. You can just pick it up again, no matter how long it's been. But no. It's more like a toolbox, and if you don't take care of your tools, if you don't sharpen them from time to time, well, eventually the tools are going to get dull."

"Hailey had a good toolbox, didn't she?" Raine ventured.

Thorne shook her head and sneered. "It wasn't that good. But it was so similar to how mine had been. Her paintings... it was like looking at what I used to paint, at what I could have painted if I hadn't been scared and taken the safer road. If you saw one of my old paintings and then saw one of hers, you'd think the same person had painted them. The only thing was, a painting by the Director of the Cascadia Art School was going to command a much higher price than the same painting from some unknown nobody. So, I made Hailey a proposal. She painted the paintings, but we sold them under my name, and split the profits. She got some much needed money, and I got some much needed recognition."

"Is it recognition if it's not really your stuff?" Sommers asked.

Thorne glared at Sommers. "I never did like you very much. You are very confident in your abilities and you have used them expertly to succeed. That's exactly what I didn't do."

"Did you kill her?" Raine asked. "Did you shoot Hailey in the heart and make it look like a suicide?"

"Oh God, no," Thorne waved away the suggestion. "That was the entire point. I wasn't about to risk murdering someone. No, I just played on her already prominent insecurities. I mean, you don't agree to let someone else put their name on your art unless you have serious self-confidence issues. When she started wavering on our arrangements, I began weekly counseling sessions with her. I made sure I knew exactly what she was thinking. Her biggest fear was not just of failing as an artist, but failing while everyone else succeeded. That gave me the idea for the gallery and I knew Duncan would agree. Really, that man is too kind for his own good. He almost lost everything because of it."

"You told her to kill herself?" Sommers asked.

"I told her it wouldn't be unheard of for an artist to take their own life," Thorne explained. "She brought the gun. She pulled the trigger. And I was there to make sure she didn't waver. It was me who went out that back door, Daniel. Except that I turned right where you turned left. I circled back to the front door and was inside again before my hair could even get wet."

"What about Veronica Kwon?" Raine asked. "That wasn't another suggested suicide. I met her. She wasn't suicidal. She was excited about her future."

Thorne laughed again. "Ah yes, I heard about your little

drugged adventure at Veronica's apartment. It's a small school. Stories travel fast, especially good ones. But you're right, I never would have been able to convince Veronica Kwon to kill herself. What did Caleb say happened?"

"He said she discovered what he'd done so he had to kill her," Raine answered, "but he was pretty vague. I don't think he even knew where the photograph of her body was taken."

"I don't think he knew we would realize he wasn't even there that night," Sommers added.

Thorne nodded. "He probably didn't. He's not actually a very smart man. The money he uses to buy entire buildings? He inherited it from his father. The only smart thing he ever did was hire a money manager to make sure he didn't blow it all on drugs and strippers. It probably never occurred to him that being called away on a business trip the night of the murder would leave receipts proving he couldn't have done it. Although, who knows? The police rarely look for exculpatory evidence, do they, Daniel?"

Raine had to agree. "Not in my experience."

"So, is that what happened?" Sommers returned to the murder itself. "Did Veronica figure out what you did and threaten to tell the police?"

"She did figure it out," Thorne agreed, "but it was my fault. I got cocky. I put up a single painting at the second exhibition. I thought I could get away with it, but Veronica recognized the style. You did too, Daniel, but you didn't realize it. I think Veronica might have even seen Hailey working on that particular painting before I signed my name to it. She didn't threaten to call the police, but I knew it was the sort of good story that would spread through the entire school within hours. I would be ruined as both an artist and a teacher. I would lose everything."

"So, you panicked and slit her throat," Raine said, "then cleaned up the mess from the struggle to cover your tracks."

Thorne frowned. "I did not panic. I took the logical steps to preserve my own position in the world. Everyone does that, Daniel. But not everyone is willing to go as far as I did."

"Yeah, so I'm just going to step outside and call the police," Sommers announced. "I'll be right back. You kids keep talking."

But Raine didn't say anything for several minutes. He didn't know what to say. Thorne had said it all. Despite everything, he was still saddened by what could have been.

"You didn't have to go so far, Selina," he finally said. "You could have come to me. That's what I do. I help people get out of trouble, and you're in a lot of trouble now. You're going to need a good lawyer. But with everything that's happened, I can't be your lawyer. I can't be your anything."

"That's okay, Daniel," she said. "You never were."

EPILOGUE

It took some time, but Finch eventually paid the last of his retainer. Raine had to go to the gallery to remind him, and pick up the check in person, but it was worth the walk. Sommers offered to meet met him there to make sure Finch closed out the account. Her presence would remind Finch that Raine was a friend of a friend, and not just some random person he had done business with. That personal connection was really all the leverage Raine had, short of suing him for the balance. He was hardly going to break Finch's hand.

"Here you are." Finch handed Raine an oversized business check made out for the balance owed. "It was a pleasure doing business with you. I hope never to see you again."

"Duncan!" Sommers chided.

"No worries," Raine said. "I get a lot of that. Comes with the job."

"That's what I meant," Finch assured.

Raine took the check, confirmed the amount was correct, then folded it and tucked it into his jacket pocket.

"I still can't believe Selina did all that." Finch shook his head. "And that she was willing to let me take the fall for it."

Raine shrugged slightly. "Well, it wasn't like you were going to prison the way Caleb would have. You just would have lost your gallery, and livelihood, and all of your assets."

"Oh, is that all?" Finch scoffed.

"At least she didn't really let Caleb take the fall," Sommers said. "She confessed."

"Because we confronted her," Raine pointed out. "I'm not sure she wasn't contemplating a one-way ticket to Rio de Janeiro."

"Is she going to fight it?" Sommers asked. "I mean, can they even charge her with Hailey's death?"

"They might be able to," Raine answered, "but they probably won't. There's a theory for manslaughter, but they'll probably just threaten her with it to get her to plead guilty to Veronica's murder. She'll get twenty years minimum for that, probably more."

"That doesn't seem like enough," Finch put in.

"It's probably not, but we don't make the sentencing laws," Raine said.

"What about Caleb?" Sommers asked. "Is he going to get charged with perjury for lying on the stand?"

Raine shook his head. "No. If they charge him, he has the right to remain silent and they can't use him to prove the case against Selina. He's more valuable to the prosecution as a witness than a codefendant. But I asked around, and apparently Caleb is paying for some high-priced defense attorney for Selina."

"Even after she let him take the blame for her?" Finch shook his head. "That doesn't make any sense."

"It makes total sense," Sommers disagreed. "And it's for

the same reason he tried to take the blame in the first place. He loved her."

"She must have loved him back," Raine found himself still a bit pained to admit. "He obviously knew the details of what had happened when he made that witness-stand confession. Selina must have confided in him."

"Guilty conscience," Sommers observed. "It always feels better to tell someone your secrets."

"A partner." Raine grinned at her.

Sommers smiled back and cocked her head at him. "Do you have any secrets you need to share with me, Mr. Raine?"

"I do have one," Raine admitted.

Sommers raised an eyebrow. "Oh yeah? What's that?"

Raine pointed across the street. "I could really go for some ice cream."

WE HOPE YOU ENJOYED THIS BOOK

If you could spend a moment to write an honest review on Amazon, no matter how short, we would be extremely grateful. They really do help readers discover new authors.

ALSO BY STEPHEN PENNER

Rain City Legal Thriller Series

Burden of Proof

Trial By Jury